CONNECTING
THE DOTS

CONNECTING THE DOTS

G.N. Harris

To order additional copies of this book, contact:
Xlibris Corporation
1-888-795-4274
www.Xlibris.com
Orders@Xlibris.com

CONTENTS

This book is for no one,
and/or everyone.

PART 1

1.

I am broke and lonely and not worth listening to. Do so at your own risk. I am mentally paralyzed. Recently I was stunned by a revelation that I call religious. I have seen a truth that will probably destroy me. I'd like to die a flaming star—burst into a phantasmagoria of color and bright burning gas. But instead I'll fizzle out and die upon infinite blackness. Yes, that's likely how it will end for me.

I'm not like you at all. I don't think the same things you do. I have inklings about the universe and the way it works. My mind tends toward deciphering age-old mysteries of the human condition most days, not what's on sale at the mall or whose CD is atop the charts. I can't even think about what I should buy. I've failed as a consumer. I'm too frugal with money. I don't want to work, and often I don't have to. My mind leads me to what I need—I might say mystically or psychically, but I believe everything is mystic and psychic so there's no use making a distinction. I'm content with what I get, though I've come close to starving on several occasions. I still do owe my last friends a considerable amount.

I'm an unusual person, all who know me would agree, though I have no friends left. It's generally understood by now that I will never change. I've mastered the unlikely trick of turning reality inside out, so that I evoke the unconscious in everyday, normal life. I reveal the seams that hold events together. Of course, I don't know how I do it, and I can't produce results on demand, so I'm often judged a kook or a fraud, eccentric or insane.

If you saw my car you'd agree. My car has become a sight—or blight, yes, that's it, a rolling blight. But it wasn't my fault the paint began peeling and a chipped and frayed look overtook the thing. Its surface became the muted gray underneath—primer—but only in patches. Part of the car looks perfect. But the patches are ragged psychedelic blots, added to a crack across the windshield and a broken-off radio antenna, just a rusted stump. Inside I'd been riding with only one radio speaker working. Songs played minus some tracks. This was all right, though. It allowed me to hear the words more clearly, without guitars and drums drowning them out. Hearing exactly what is said is essential to me, just as seeing precisely what is visible also is, as I will explain to you, in detail.

My car situation was quite bizarre but I had no money to fix anything—the radio or the engine—just enough to push on, deteriorating, wearing down, breaking apart, and losing wheels. I knew the thing was going to die, but it kept choking and lived.

I had no embarrassment, no shame about any of this. I accepted my general condition and the nature of things. I had to give up notions of embarrassment. It couldn't exist for me. I was beyond embarrassment. I felt a certain humiliation, it's true, but it blended well with me. If anything, I'd learned that it was all right to be the smallest thing. The smallest thing was important, too. I'd likened it to a rosary. I'd flashed upon what a rosary bead meant. I compared myself to a rosary bead. We were both the smallest things. But we were okay. We were important, too. We were vested with the sacred. I thought of how a prayer on a rosary bead was complete concentration. Total faith put in a tiny piece of wood or plastic, which transformed the bead. It became a catalyst for cosmic sleight-of-hand. (You know what I mean by that, don't you—how some ordinary, mundane action can, at times, produce wonders.) I, too, was a catalyst—a bead vested with cosmic awareness. I just had to contemplate myself in a particular way to get results. Because, you see, I am at its mercy, the cosmos I mean. The cosmos is a tricky thing, a tricky place. It is both a thing and a place. It is a living thing, a being I should say—and it "be" everywhere, as any rapper would tell you.

My ego is not invested in my car. I don't see the car as my identity or a reflection of me. I am not what I drive. Some former friends suggested I get it painted. I ask you, would I be a different person the day of its painting? Would I change? Would a presentable car make all the difference? Could I expect myself to feel more presentable as well? Would a new coat of paint create a renewed self-image? I could drive smiling, then, right? I would feel welcome in traffic. Perhaps I should just paint myself. I was obviously not welcome in traffic as it was, judging from the frowns and stares I got. But it didn't matter. I didn't have enough for a can of spray let alone the price of a paint job. Anyway, I was on the inside, enjoying other people's colored car bodies, unable to see my own.

Besides, I didn't need extra torment. I was in an agitated state already, restless due to a ticket I'd gotten that was unfair. I'd gone to the ticket window at city hall several times to protest it. They sent me around to several other stops, other windows at the offices, all in a circle that led me back to the first window where I'd started. Only, when I finally returned all the way to the first window, the woman I'd spoken to—an alluring Asian lady in a red dress—wasn't there. She didn't even work there anymore. Only several days later, and there was no record of my visit. The ticket was unfair, it doesn't matter how, and I don't even have to tell you how. But I was upset and distressed far beyond what I should have been.

I was also physically affected by my landlady's demands. I had been avoiding her, but for good reason. She had overcharged me. The room I occupied was slovenly, in need of repair, and she refused to fix it. Then she came yapping and complaining for her rent. My heartbeats raced and sweat droplets formed around my neck and under my arms. My stomach contracted into a pit-sized tablet of anxiety. I had all my arguments clear in my head, but I worried that, confronting her, my words would mangle and sputter. I'd grow upset and yell, shake and tremble with too much excitement, while she would stand firm, calm, a creeping, crooked grin spreading while she watched me destroy myself.

We had gotten off to a poor start. My name is Flex Ponderosa. I will not try to tell you it's my real name. I have long since forgotten my real name. I chose Flex Ponderosa because of its bigness, the expanse, and also its association with muscles, body work, hard physical tautness, dynamic muscular imagery mixed with a place from a popular television show about rugged, free spirited cowboys. To me, it all said openness, exercise of the mind, big ideas. That is, until I told her—the landlady—my name. "Flecks, like little flecks of dirt," she misinterpreted. So you ponder flecks of dirt. How funny!" All right if, in her mind I was a fleck, just the smallest thing, to be brushed off, all right then. Even the smallest thing, even a fleck I'd learned, was okay.

But it's true I wanted to be big. Let me correct that. I was big, at times. I am both big and small. That is my problem. But it's not just my problem; it's yours, too. How? you ask. Because when I am small I am only myself, but when I am big I am everyone, including you. Understand? Of course you don't. But the nature of bigness and smallness is important to me. Expansion and contraction is how the soul operates, I think. I have been reduced to a mite in the scheme of things, but I also *am* the scheme of things. Understand? Of course you don't. Where do I end and you begin, I might rephrase it. The line is constantly moving; sometimes it disappears. I know what it is to be trapped inside the dimensions of a subatomic particle, still aware. I also know how it feels to be unending light over a horizon, unbounded, silly with glee— existence a cake-like aroma wafting everywhere. This dual nature confronts me everyday. Little me aspires to be big me, and big me can't accept himself. That's why I call myself Flex Ponderosa. I am a little man who knows how big reality is, but can't remain that big, and so must carry a second identity like a reminder. When I state my name aloud it puffs me up, makes me remember, that there is no end. Life is a landscape dream. There's my name in lights on a billboard in the desert.

I ignored the landlady's mocking of my name but I couldn't ignore her faulty accounting. The room I rented was in a large house, the size of a castle, with multiple boarders. I didn't even know how many others lived there. But the one bulb I burned and the few showers I took could not possibly add up to the sum she charged me. I disputed the amount, didn't have it to pay, I told her. Notices in red letters appeared tacked in the hallway. Raps on my door at two a.m. woke me with the ultimatum to pay or move. The new month approached and I didn't have the rent. Home life, even the thought of it, tensed me, yet I tried to hold onto that room. I admit I did it because I thought I could. New people came and went and rooms stood empty for stretches. I was prepared to slip into a different one for a night, and then another if I had to. But tiptoeing about I found she kept them all securely locked.

With no free access to my room, I had to keep on the move. My eating habits suffered. I was eating horrid slop, instant meals out of an envelope, fast food and often nothing at all. I forgot to eat for long stretches, complete days, unable to recall when I'd last had a bite and even unable to decide if I was hungry. But when I finally gave in I ingested packages of artificial foodstuff, chunks of cardboard flavored lab experiments in decorated cellophane. Shortly after I'd have all kinds of cramps and bloating, stomach pain and illness, so that my body temperature rose and I sweated and wretched. No matter, I'd stuff myself full of the same crap again later, to save pennies (the smallest, most underrated currency, God's coins I call them) just so long as there was something in me, anything, short of dirt or poison.

And I drove. I drove and stopped, drove and stopped, that old unsightly car, still rolling despite its scabs. I was unable to actually go in anywhere. That's right, I'd drive to my destination, a club or movie or restaurant, and then sit stupidly in the parking lot for thirty minutes, an hour, paralyzed with anxiety. I didn't know anyone and wouldn't last long in there I told myself. I'd have to spend what money I had left, and the time would tick so slowly. I'd talk to no one and no one would talk to me. In minutes I'd feel sufficiently invisible as the yapping social dancers chattered, glancing past me, ignoring me. I couldn't do it. I told you, I am not like you.

I sat in my monstrous, atrocious car thinking what I should do, until patrons leaving and walking to their own cars—clean shiny things of beauty and status—noticed me. And I'd just be sitting there, staring. I'm waiting for someone, I'd tell myself. What are you looking at? I'd wonder at their glances and curious peeks. Can't you see I'm relaxing for a moment before a long drive to pick up relatives who are staying the week with me? What do you think I'm doing sitting here? Do you think I have nowhere to go?

I developed a new way of coming and going to parking lots. True, I no longer actually got out of my car. But I pretended I had. It was simple. I'd pull up to a movie theater, stop and park, wait. Then in a while, I'd pull out and leave, just ahead of the exiting crowd. But not as if I'd just sat there. No, I'd leave as if coming from a movie. What a good movie, I'd think, very satisfied. The action and drama and especially the romance were marvelous. I'd feel a bond with the hero, as moviegoers do, and his identity would rub off on me. The world would look new, different, for now I was seeing it through the eyes of a modern, lovable character that had admirable traits and was important in the scheme of things. Yes, I'd just seen a movie and the feelings from it lingered for hours.

The same with restaurants, as I'd pull away with the idea of a full course meal, a relaxed, pleasurable time in good company, dining and drinking. Yes, I never left anywhere without favorable impressions and memories now, though I never actually went in anywhere.

I did get out, though, in public parks, provided there was no one about and I could sit alone, in peace. Trees and grass were all I needed and sometimes a bench. Then I could sit for hours not even thinking. In fact, I'd decided there was no difference between me and a cat. I simply looked, wide-eyed, at nature, cars going by, little movements about me of birds and wind in branches and occasional passersby. Yes, I was a cat, at least, as far as intelligence and social action, at least a cat.

I had an observation while I sat and stared like a cat. (So, I was above a cat after all!) My observation was—hope and despair are incremental terms; things take a turn for the worse or better and proceed from there, slowly, not suddenly like catastrophe or joy.

2.

I must reassert my name. It's Flex Ponderosa and it's significant. You see my real name has no class. No classification. No identity as anybody or even as a thing. I'm a nothing, a mite, aspiring to be a dust ball. But Flex Ponderosa covers a canvas of western plains, with hills. It's vast in its imagery and implication. I'm like a supercharged person with that name. What it really represents is my ambition. A name like that fulfills my ambition. I am important with a name like that. I have attained a status above the normal, beyond the routine. Isn't that what you, what everybody wants— to attain a status above it all? We want to be able to boast of our big achievements. What could be a bigger boast than to claim you know it all, the truth of existence, the mystery behind creation?! Or, even to have a clue, a valid hint of the truth about the real state of things—that's status, that's standing. Then you can make statements about what all of this is, what we're doing here. (Actually, you can be a blithering idiot and still claim to have it all figured out, and guaranteed, legions will believe you, attend your seminars, buy your books, stand in line to touch you.) Isn't that the only thing that's really going on—we're here and we don't have a real idea why and we know we can't figure it out, but we wonder if there is someone out there who has the answer (the secret) to what it's all for and what it's about. Well, my adopted name suggests that I am that person.

Unfortunately, I have social inertia. That sets me apart and keeps me there, the feeling of inertia at my core. It keeps me from making contact. I have long since lost contact with the world. What is it you're all doing, anyway? Are you like me at all?

Lately I have convinced myself that just existing is exquisite and special. But I have a grander delusion, that I am a blessed entity. If I can't quite picture myself with a halo, I at least detect a glow coming from me. It's holy. I could be sacred. There must be, simply must be more to who I am, what I am, what's going on here than a job and a title and a salary.

How do you all do it? How do you decide to be an office manager or a butcher? Are you forced into it? How did it get to be what you wanted, while you're here being a potential sacred being? Do you see what I mean? I'm thinking of myself as a sacred entity, and then I'm filling out an application to work part-time at Burger King. How did such a gulf come to exist in every day? Each day unfolds with that dichotomy. I approach the world as a unique sentient being and must settle in comfortably with the business of life. I suspect my approach is wrong. Truly now, how many of you think of yourselves as unique sentient beings when you awake and stare out at the surroundings each dawn?

3.

I have recently ceased being what is called normal. I have seen beyond normal and I suppose there's no going back. I don't know how I did it, how I peered through some tiny crack in the big picture, but there's no denying it now. I see that the life I'd been living, the lives we all lead, are hilariously ignorant. I don't mean that as an insult, I just don't know how else to put it. You've heard how scientists say we really only use ten percent of our brains? Well, I'm certain I've stumbled upon at least the eleventh percent. I can't claim any more than that, really, but I'm ready to stand up and assert at least eleven percent, I'll bet my life on it. The funny thing, and also a most compelling fact, is that the eleventh percent was right in front of my eyes the whole time, just as I'm certain the rest of it—twelve to one hundred percent of the brain's potential—is also staring me in the face.

What does that mean? What kind of abnormal state have I realized? It only means that it's still the same world. But my open eyes perceive it differently now. I'm no longer separate (I never was!). I may be alienated, isolated, desolate, desperate and alone. But I exist always and forever (and will always be, I must emphasize that, for we tend to use the word 'always' as if it had a temporary application that ends after a few decades or with a life, just as 'forever' isn't good enough at the end of prayers, but must be augmented ' and ever', you see, as if just forever is not long enough and needs an extra 'ever' to ensure we mean for all time, for eternity, world without end, on and on). Yes, I've seen beyond and understand myself to be a dot in a grand picture. I'm intent now on visualizing the complete scene; like a children's dot-to-dot, it's that simple. I have a small idea, a notion that's all, that this grand picture, this design once I perceive it fully, will be the other eighty-nine percent of the brain's function. It will be vast and awesome, a monstrous miracle unfathomable from my current point of view. It will transform me completely from what I think I am into something mighty, omniscient and omnipresent. In doing so it will completely erase the dichotomy of existence, the feeling of being a separate entity within a mysterious, unknowable universe. Then I'll become what I suspect I truly am.

Let me tell you this inkling I have about who I truly am.

Speaking from my current, pint-sized position of powerlessness I see it this way. I'm an integral part of a larger, vast interconnected reality that affects me profoundly in and throughout its every action and movement. Its scope is so immense and overall being so impressive that I cannot fathom its totality. I cannot discern its every nuance and influence on my moment-to-moment existence. In fact, of this monstrous form that seems to contain me and even be dependent on me for at least a few square feet of its expression, I can only see a little bit, a minuscule portion of the whole. Its endless body extends and expands in every direction away from me. Every point—every dot—of this Reality is conscious. Every degree of longitude and latitude is alive. All the dots together comprise one whole huge being. And I am a dot of this infinite picture. Added up, though, at the sum of its parts, this whole huge being is a tricky, unfathomable presence.

I am at its mercy.

It's all controlling in its chaos. There's no one or nothing in charge of this series of interconnected dots happening against a background. But the whole of it is alive and conscious, including the background. Most of us are comfortable with the idea of an authority figure in the sky that knows it all. We expect someone (a being on a cloud) to have the answers. I'm sorry to destroy notions of comfort, but there's no one overruling force or vision, no wise compassionate council of moralists keeping watch—only an ever-fluctuating stream of events and coincidences impossible to control. Go ahead, look to a preacher or a president, a savior, someone human or invisible, to preside over a "somewhere" where it's all right and orderly. That desire stems from fear, fear of the unknown, fear of what's "out there." We sense—even as we ride about in luxury cars, talking on cell phones, wired in by remote to our security system at home, covered by life and accident insurance, carrying a loaded pistol in the glove compartment—we sense that it is too far out of our control. We sense that the vast interconnectedness (even if we don't think of it as connected) is, at too many junctures, wild and unpredictable, dangerous and death inducing, that it knows no fairness. (Life isn't fair, we've all heard that one, especially when someone less deserving gets a promotion or attains celebrity status.) Yes, we pray to an invisible god to protect us, expect elected leaders to smooth the way, and rely upon scientists and experts (there are no experts, in anything) to provide answers. But just beneath the surface—the surface of our mind (the same as the surface of our world)—our intuition tells us we're buying time, skating on thin ice (another one we've heard and nod our heads at, not knowing its accuracy). Really, we don't have the answers; we don't even know the question. We're hopelessly alone and vulnerable (though this last notion takes courage, true self-examination to admit, and can be ignored and covered up over the course of a lifetime by scheduling social events, working overtime and keeping busy). Well, what to do? What to do? Start by admitting we're hopeless, alone and vulnerable. Humble our selves to the awe each day, each moment of consciousness elucidates. Perhaps in that way we can carve out a more harmonious union between the vast unknown and our little selves (as if one was not composed of the other). At least it's worth a try. Otherwise the fear rules our lives, even as we claim dominance over fear, superiority over puny fear. I know because I was once as afraid as anyone. But I have seen now that there is nothing to be afraid of, nothing to lose, because there is nothing to have, nothing to attain, and nowhere else to be.

Fear is gone from me and I have one friend, the great good sky and the surrounding cosmos. It is a companion to me. I take some solace knowing that it will always be there. I will never actually be alone. There will always be a planet off in the night distance, or a tree nearby. Truly I cannot be lost, ever. Overall, I am at home wherever I am, wherever I go. This friend of mine provides for me, but is also dangerous. It is generous and then it might kill me. I am like a little puppet it can push around or a puppy it will pet and wean. Perhaps my own general entertainment value determines whether I am fed or murdered. I try to remain in good graces with the world at large. I barter a daily existence by maintaining a humor and remaining wry and humble. So far I think it likes me, enough to tolerate my idiosyncrasies at least, enough not to punish me too severely. I have struck a bargain with it and so it tickles me daily, and I jump. Together we go down the road as one.

Part of its horrific, absurd scenario is that I will experience a death. I have no problem with that. I have a problem with the life I've awakened into, not the death that, by necessity, must follow. Commonly, what we hope to do in life is dress well, eat well, drive an expensive car, live in a big beautiful house, have lots of friends and admirers, keep a large supply of money in the bank, do lots of business and shop. If we can't do these things we instead spend our time on this planet, in this life, trying to do these things. So, the ones who try, spend much time working at tasks and jobs they despise, and most of them never get anywhere, just continue along "trying" for the desired life. They dress passably, eat fast food and microwave dinners, make car payments and get needed repairs. They live in cramped apartments and modest rental houses, worry that their friends might be doing better than them, put away funds for a rainy day or their kids' education or retirement. But sometimes they have to withdraw a part to bail Uncle Ed out of jail or loan the brother-in-law the gas bill. They worry that their jobs will be eliminated or business will fall off and so put in overtime and weekends. They buy everything on sale, even if it was drastically marked up just a week prior and then "reduced" for one day only.

What does death mean? It waits around every corner. It could all be over at any moment. One day you're fine and the next you have cancer. Or you're walking and part of a building topples and crushes you. Or some driver simply veers one foot from the path they're traveling at seventy miles an hour and your life is over. That's how fragile you are. You zoom along your jolly way with sudden death lurking all about you. You are on your way to go shopping, or to dine at a fabulous restaurant, or to take thousands of dollars from the bank. Then, splat, you are squashed like a bug by an out-of-control semi. What then of the dining and shopping? Well, they are left to someone else. Such are the pleasures of life. In the midst of life's pleasures, you die. It will always be so. Pleasures you have not partaken of will exist, will be all around you, will still be beckoning with neon signs and half-off stickers as you expire, one hand extended to the nearest rack of clearance items. Such is the all-consuming lure of what it is we're told to keep busy with in this life. We are consumed by our consumerism. We know we're going to die. No one ever forgets. Yet, we must, yes, yes we must have that shirt or that jacket or the latest computer or sleekest car. We've even coined an expression—"To die for!" referring to the worth of some material item. That coat or that stereo or even that bracelet, I would give my life for. Now, that's shopping.

Why can't I be like that? Was I born with some defect of mind or soul, some gap of understanding when it comes to what is really worth my time and attention? Why do I settle for the barest necessities without care, while all about me are souls whose eyes light up at the sight of sports cars and elegant sofas? Well, to tell you the truth I was like that once, briefly, or at least I thought I was like that. I did my best to join in, be one of you, earn and spend, earn and spend. But no use, ultimately, I was exposed for the misfit I've always been. But we'll get to that. In the meantime, don't think I'm unhappy because I own nothing. I don't hold a grudge. I don't lament not being a rabid consumer. I have already said that all things are metaphysical, so objects, too, must be metaphysical, and having them is no harm. Someone has to have them. They are everywhere. The stuff of life and the world and our bodies is all physical, not different from the stuff of sports cars and elegant sofas. It is the same to have one as to have the other—the same, exactly the same, to have a shiny Mercedes as it is to have a stalled Ford—so why not have the better vehicle? With the better vehicle you get around in life, travel fast and whoosh right by slower drivers, cause heads to turn to look at you because you're in this impressive collection of parts. You get where you're going in life, able to provide cushioned comfort and top performance for your passengers. In the stalled Ford, you are left by the roadside as the world passes you by; you get nowhere in life. You do, though, cause heads to turn—to curse you—and you have no passengers, or scoffing unhappy ones.

But, suppose you are going nowhere in life. Ah, what then? Suppose you've seen through this idea that there is anywhere to go or anything to attain. Suppose you know that one place is the same as another, that traveling is the same as arriving, that there is no hurry to get to your death, it will come quickly enough. What do you do then, when you have put the same value on all things, and nothing is better or worse than anything else?

Could you accept that the only reason to be here is to tell others you love them? What if that is the sole and singular purpose to having this physical incarnation—to, ironically—realize you are a spiritual entity—that we all are—and to tell each other "I love you." Without that, what good is a death? So Mom or Pop goes to the grave after a life of hard work and modest means, and leaves a small sum for the children. Is the deceased person like a file? We can close the book on that one, tally up the final total, assess a value—how much earned, how much spent, how much accumulated, how much lost or squandered—and then move on, invest, vacation, watch the game, have a baby. Did we forget something? Did we tell the deceased person we loved them? Yes, yes, we did, at the last moment, on the death bed, as they reeled incoherent and squinted through glazed over eyes at unrecognized relatives, their bones frail and shaky, their skin peeling off, their teeth rotted out, their lungs gasping, their heart failing, then we said it. Before that? Well, yes, on certain holidays and Christmas, always on Christmas, and in long-distance phone conversations. And did we realize what we meant when we said it those times? Or has it become such an expected platitude that we mouthed it, and pronounced it, and even felt something behind it, but didn't really say it, for all of time and eternity (forever and ever) and this moment, I love you. If not, why not? Could it be that we did not know ourselves as spiritual beings and could not express love as the only thing, the one and only true thing, the essential element of life and existence. Yes, it could be that we've become enslaved to Hallmark meanings of what love is, and that we don't know how deep love runs, and that love is the only reason to suffer a life.

4.

Sometimes it shows me signs, directs me where to go. I keep my sixth sense fine tuned for just such omens and occurrences. I desperately need them. I count on them. Without them I am stymied. I cannot navigate. That is what I have been reduced to, cutting a path through reality. I steer with clues provided by the one mind. They are usually not monumental; they are slight things, often nearly unnoticeable. They are always and can only be very personal. No one else could know what these clues mean, because they are the visible representation of the inside of my head. I see that a lot. I don't know precisely what it means. I have not connected all the dots. I believe anyone who thinks they have connected the dots to be mistaken. Not because it can't be done, but because I am one of the dots and so are you. I don't know how it all works, but I am a dot in it. Perhaps it was as a dot, or someone who feels himself to be the equivalent of a dot, that I made the association of a gnat.

When I'd first moved to the room, I adopted a gnat as my companion. A gnat flits aimlessly like I do. It's the smallest thing, the most insignificant, except to me. I noticed it in the thin light when I came in from the empty day. When the day emptied out, I don't know. People fell away and I was left with the gnat. I came home to this bouncy black dot—so bouncy it overjoyed me. I wanted to name the gnat and even wondered what to feed it. But that was stupid. A gnat could pause on a crumb or near a drop of spilled milk, couldn't it? It occurred to me that I'd never seen a gnat eat. But I believed them to be self-supporting—a pet that cared for itself. But I wanted to care for it.

It's not so silly to think of befriending a gnat. That's a reasonable alternative to a solitary person. The most outlandish behavior always comes down to the state of mind of the individual caught in the circumstances that caused the behavior. That's how horrible crimes, minor injustices, moral transgressions, and the like, that shock us, can all be explained. You had to be there, psychologically. Acts considered irrational to most become the norm for sad, demented psyches that have wandered into inescapable states of mind. And that's what everything is—a state of mind. My own describes an empty flat of existence, vacant except for me, me everywhere. At the same time, I have realized how important it is to express this universal love I'm now aware of. Kind of a ridiculous quagmire isn't it? I peer in for the signpost that will lead me to her, that beautiful creature of softness who will soothe reality, show me how it sparkles and shines, how reality will bend to my wishes and jump when I say so, put on a magic show and perform all the tricks it knows just for me, for us. I'm talking about a woman, of course. I stared an extra moment at the alluring Asian woman in the red dress at the wrong City Hall window where I went to protest my ticket. I wondered if she was a sign (a welcoming sign) but I couldn't get any words out, no real words, just stammering about my ticket and how unfair it was. I'm sure she thought me a total fool but thinking about her later I was certain I'd overlooked an obvious omen—that I was about to have a relationship, with her. Of course, it was clear in my head afterwards. Her bright dress made her stand out against the drab background of other city workers. For an instant she had diverted my anxiety from my ticket. But just as quickly it had turned into anxiety over speaking to her. I kept my remarks proper and within the boundaries of discussing the reason I'd been ticketed and how it was a mistake, and she seemed sympathetic, I'm sure she did. She even seemed sincere when she sent me along to another window and I'm positive—yes, positive—that she could not have known that it, too, would be the wrong window, and that I would circle about, from room to room in that great old City Hall building until I ended back at her window. (It even occurred to me, in my frantic, souped-up state, that she arranged it that way, to see me again. Do you see how

states of mind can lead to astonishing misinterpretations of events?)
When at last, after a slew of visits, I was directed back to where I'd
started (I never thought of going back to her window on my own,
to chat, to get to know each other) I actually approached her window
with glee, not thoughts of ironing out a legal issue. I listened to
the echo of my own footsteps in the cavernous hallway that led to
her, excitedly wondering what she'd be wearing. And then, and
then . . . she wasn't there. A different woman, older, with bristly
gray hair, glasses and a scowl met me. So she had not been an
omen after all, and my life of talking to myself went on.

Such is the oblivion that led me to the gnat. I had already
stopped killing the crawlers and creepers that I encountered in my
room. In a life full of relationships, busy with worldly concerns
and shopping, I would have stamped their lives out without a
thought. But they had become company and several times I found
myself looking around for them when none showed.

Then I lost the gnat. It was gone. I don't know what a gnat's
life span is, but it couldn't be long. I looked everywhere and waited
with the light on but there was no sign of him. It occurred to me
that if a gnat appeared then, how would I know it was the same
gnat? Are there differences between gnats? Probably only another
gnat can tell. They all flit alike, I suppose. Individual traits would
be difficult to point out. Yes, he seemed to be gone, perhaps
somewhere on the rug like another speck of dirt, accidentally ground
into the carpet by my own foot.

I focused afterwards on a speck of dust in my room. I never
saw it materialize, but there it was one day, a speck. Strangely, that
speck of dust became a thought. It was an undefined thought, so
it still looked like nothing more than a dust ball. But it grew,
almost imperceptibly, like a thought. On the outside it appeared
disgusting, gray matter and thread curled together. Inside you
could not tell exactly what litter comprised it, but it suggested
something distasteful. I had the fascinating, lucid feeling that I
was peering at a corner of my own mind, watching an idea generate.

I fantasized that my one thought would lead me to fame and

fortune (such is the daily dream of the poor). It had to be an important thought, one that had never been thought before, a new thought. I put that kind of concentration into the speck of dust I was monitoring. I watched it for a long time. I don't know how long I watched it. But I'm sure I saw it move. Well, I can't say moved, but trembled, at least quivered. What is the term to use when a wisp shifts? Does it seem petty to focus attention on a puffball the size of a mite? Understand the meaning involved and the value becomes clear. My thought was growing.

The lure of wealth causes us to compromise our thinking. We devalue anything but mass market thinking, for fear it will isolate us, and we won't share in the big material pie. Then we are all starved for true sustenance, true life affirming and mind-nourishing ideas. A beach house, a new car, a high-powered stereo, the latest fashions, these are important. A new idea, and worse yet, an unproven, untested idea, not a popular, mass-market idea, is more than a waste of time. It's a threat to security. In today's world, most people ignore ideas. They turn on the TV, or go shopping, or have lunch, or set their nose to the grindstone and don't look up until a pleasing numerical figure has been transferred from a company account to their personal one. When they've run out of work or leisure activities they wonder why life is boring. Inside they have a hunger, but they don't know what for.

I am not viewed as someone who represents a new way of thinking and perceiving. I am not someone with a new door to open. I have no compelling alternative to your way of living. I am a poor, useless out-of-the-mainstream fellow who would do everyone a favor by dropping his facade of "new thinking." Stop monitoring a speck of dust and get a good paying job.

But I was confident my new idea would save me. This same overall, all-over weaving of reality—the magic carpet of existence, everything and everyone a thread—that overwhelmed, overturned and plunged me into daily consternation, would surely save me, too. My faith was in it. That "greater-than-me" (that also contained me) would shift in my favor. My new thought, was the beginning of all that.

5.

Thoughts are all around us. The visible world is the concrete representation of our minds—the inside come to life on the outside, at least that's what I think. The mind is not only inside the head; it is also outside. I know it sounds funny, but I am walking around inside my own head.

I won't force my concepts and theories down your cerebrum. You have a right to dismiss me, and my chatter; that's what most people do. I have made it clear already that I'm not like you—even though we are intimately and infinitely connected throughout all time and space. I am a misfit of sorts. You probably find my kind of thinking alarming and, most of all, unnecessary. But I mean it when I say the inside and the outside are one. All minds are connected in thought—are only pure thought—and the physical world is the sensual, touchable dimension of thought, understand?

But figuring out exactly how it all works can be nerve wracking. I admit I am as yet unable to connect the dots. Funny, you see, all the dots are already connected. There's a connection between every single thing. I don't know if people perceive the connections all around them. A man once said to me that he didn't believe in God because he didn't see any evidence that God existed. I said all I see is evidence of God. There isn't one thing that isn't evidence.

But I am unable to figure out exactly how it all works. My speck of dust is a new start, though. I take some small consolation in knowing that I have begun. My speck is born of all that has come before, all that I have learned. It will pickup momentum, grow into . . . something, an explanation, a mystery unraveled, a revelation. It's the same thing you—we all—are attempting with computer technology.

We have learned how to access and control the purely mental state on computer screens, which I know something about, though I don't own a computer and can't afford the connection fee. More and more we facilitate the manipulation of thought, interact with it, process more and greater volumes of information. But really, what are we doing? We are leaving the physical for a metaphysical experience. It is not a scary, out-of-body, inexplicable phenomenon (nothing psychic or mind-altering). No, it's a connection we can trust. We have the tool now (not ourselves, not our mind) that is on sale everywhere. It is certified safe and guaranteed to provide the desired elements on the (metaphysical) menu. Our computers, with their databases all linked to one another, are the embodiment of our thought.

Our vast frontier in the den is our connection to endless minutiae, every idea throughout all time, all the past, present and speculations on the future, every category, every theory, including personal opinions, lies and truth, sports statistics, facts and figures of every kind, and all the forbidden, the lascivious, the perverse as well. It's all there, the complete gray matter currently residing in everyone's heads, the inside of my mind and yours, the text of all of history, all the forgotten stuff even, now on record, and new conjecture aided by the assimilation of all that already exists. Be prepared. We are moving toward a program option that processes, calculates, analyzes and produces one answer, one answer to it all, after being fed and programmed all the known data in the universe.

But, of course, all of this is nothing more than what you yourself (and me) are capable of doing in our own mind(s). Our minds are equivalent to microchips containing all the known data in the (unknown) universe. But accessing it is another matter all together, something that's complete on the inside and we are trying to make complete on the outside. But just as with the outside we've conjured so far—our outside mind of shopping and traveling and entertainment—so the inside mind, our computer connection, is like a mental mall of games and distractions, sexy sideshows and fancy lighted web sites designed to keep us moving, busy, gathering and disseminating all things human, even though we've left the purely physical human realm for a trip into cyber space. Yes, even when we leave the body behind, we do the same things, and we ultimately must bring the results back to the body. So web-crawling shopping sprees result not just in new cosmic awareness, and new thought, but also in a new outfit or a new high-tech goodie delivered to your door. The worldwide web is courtesy of that same service provider that gave rise to the sun and puts fruit trees within reach. More sensual gratification, this time in the disguise of interactive thought.

The sly aspect of the computer-generated mass connection of the new century, the subtle truth, is that it demonstrates we're all one mind and can tap into ourselves anywhere, anytime, at any point, all down the (on-)line. I say demonstrates because that's what it is—a demo model. We were and always have been and always will be all one mind. But our computer hookup allows us to better understand that concept. Just put all your thoughts, data, info bytes, secrets, codes, imaginations, ruminations, theories, concepts plans and ideas—everything you can think of really, don't leave one thing out, not even crimes or misdeeds or evil plots or doughnut binges or walking the dog or a two-pack-a-day habit—on the worldwide web, and anticipate that everyone else will, too, and there you have it, a receptacle for the one mind.

This might seem to take quite a commitment, and a lot of time (which none of us have). I offer a simpler, more reasonable, yet perhaps more difficult-to-accept alternative. Join the circle of minds hooked up purely by ideas. This is beyond cyber space, more than on-line. It's the first and the final database, not electronics driven, but organic. You are the hardware and mind is the software. It begins with a speck of dust.

6.

I haven't touched anyone in a month. I am going out today to touch another person. I wonder what will happen. You can't just go touching people. They don't like it. Not only that, but I don't like it. It's just that, I think I need it. I probably need a real touch, from a person I feel close to. But there is no one like that, so I will settle for a touch from a stranger, I think. This is a difficult matter. What kind of a touch from a stranger could do me good? Perhaps if a stranger touches me, or I touch a stranger, that person will no longer be a stranger. Perhaps a connection will form. A touch could do that. It's very personal. But there are impersonal touches, as when you brush someone in a supermarket aisle or getting on a bus. In those instances you just ignore it, or apologize. Those touches do not count as real touches. In fact, they are intrusions. Some people recoil or stare or get angry if they're touched accidentally. But I won't do this. Today I will allow myself to be touched accidentally. I may even stand in a crowded place just so that will happen. I don't mean anything sexual by it. Some people equate touching with sex. That's not what I'm doing here.

You might consider this an unusual goal to leave the house with. Mine would not be the only unusual goal. Some people head out with murder in mind, or to shoot BBs through store windows as a prank, or to buy tools and materials for a home improvement project they'll never get around to, or to look in the sky for UFOs. Compared to their delinquent and ridiculous pursuits, mine is not so foolish. But it's such a small, intimate goal, so personal and also associated directly with the body that I wonder—if we did have thought police—is it an idea I'd be arrested for?

I decided to amend my thought just a bit. I was not out only to touch someone (for, no matter what I thought, the implications in this were too crude, lascivious even, nothing innocent about it at all), but I was out to make a friend.

Yes, I decided a friend was necessary, more than necessary, important really. I needed a friend. I'd had friends before, it's true, or at least I'd thought they were friends. Where had they gone, I wondered. My thought was amended. I had set out to make a friend. It seemed like an easy task. After all, there were people everywhere, just everywhere. You couldn't avoid them. They got in the way of things, caused lines to be too long and took up all the seats on the bus. But now I had a different perspective on the zillions of ant-like creatures that buzzed and flitted here and there on sidewalks and in malls—any one of them could be my friend, any one of them could turn out to be a special creature, a likeable soul, an ear, a shoulder, someone to share the burden, a cohort, a partner to drink wine and have lively discussions under the stars, or even to watch TV together. People were marvels, unique, and they made time pass more quickly. Why shouldn't I have one? There was no need to be silent, no need to keep thoughts to myself. I could make a friend out of the many hundreds passing by. A simple wave, gesture or smile would start it all. How easy! Why hadn't I thought of it before? I practically leaped off the sidewalk thinking of it.

At heart, I wanted a woman. I knew that. Still, an idea had formed that I needed to be open to all of mankind. The first touch need not be the vital one, the crucial one that might grow into a relationship. That first touch was to warm me up, get me into the flow, into the game. The icebreaker, that's what they called it. In that analogy, my world was Antarctica, a sheet of frozen reality I couldn't break through.

Then I saw her. The Asian woman was coming toward me, there, right out on the city sidewalk in the bright light of day. She was not in the red dress this time, but a gray one-piece that hugged her and slid this way and that with her shifting torso. She was sexier and more desirable even than before. Most importantly, she was within reach. She was there to touch. Admittedly, I was excited. I cán't deny I wanted suddenly more than a friendly touch. Yes, my modest goal to touch someone had been transformed in a moment, at one sight of her. There was no time to consider the moral implications. She was right there, in front of me. Our eyes met, locked, and . . . the Asian woman only looked at me as she passed. She didn't recognize me. I said nothing, but pulled the crumbling parking ticket from my pocket. She didn't notice or acknowledge it. Did parking tickets mean nothing to her now that she no longer worked at the City Hall window? Maybe it wasn't even her, I mused when she was far down the block.

A touch would come. It was better if I let it happen of itself. Perhaps someone would touch me. I remained on the sidewalk. But it wasn't a busy day. Not many people were out. No one came close to me. I turned and headed aimlessly (like a gnat) in no direction. My goal to touch someone, transformed into my goal to make a friend, seemed transparent and worthless. I was not out shopping. I didn't have any money. I felt I had no legitimate reason to be on the sidewalk.

7.

I dreamed I was bodiless and floating down a long tunnel, leading to something I knew was essential, miraculous. The passageway went on, a porthole through time and space, and far, far at the end I discerned a little figure beckoning to me. At first, it appeared as only the slightest movement of something so small . . . a finger crooking, motioning me toward it. Was that it? I kept moving closer, but it seemed a long way off, far enough away for the passage of a million different thoughts before I reached it. Briefly, it shocked me. It became the lascivious finger of an unseen leering face, and its curling motion was sexual, disgusting. Just as suddenly it became, for a moment, not a finger but a baseball bat being swung, but who was doing the swinging? That notion had only taken hold when the tiny, slightly moving object again shifted shape. It seemed that each time I got close, my consciousness saw through the form I'd ascribed to it, and it appeared further from me once again, and I'd return to trying to determine exactly what it was. It wriggled and squirmed, but in no hurry. It seemed to have a consciousness behind it that was somehow accommodating. Was I the only differential here? Was it up to me to give this little repeat motion object its definition? Yes, that was it! It dawned on me all at once and I heard a voice say "Very good," as if I'd learned a lesson. At that second, I arrived at the end of the tunnel and squealed with laughter. The tiny twitching object at the end of the long continuous path was my own finger, tickling myself!

Oh what a metaphor! I saw it all, and clearly. I was the only thing behind everything. I was the man behind the curtain. Every notion that entered my mind, passed through me, was acted upon by me or ignored, was placed there by me. I was the programmer, as well as the program. I was the doctor operating upon myself. I invented the agenda and I carried it out. I created the world and I inhabited it. Not only that, but I put up the curtain of illusion, and I was the audience clapping madly at the show! King and fool, I was both. Executioner and victim, I was both. Puppet and string-puller, I was both.

The voice that had commented, "Very good," had been my voice, inside my head. But it came from outside my head. What did that tell me? That I was outside my head. That I was much more than I'd previously thought I was. I was bigger, grander. I was immense. I was all things, unlimited, unbounded, without end. I was the whole pod pretending it was only the pea. What a game!

8.

I awoke feeling small, trapped by my body. I understood that I was everything, all things, but I appeared to be the same isolated individual as on other days. I remained alert to the sound of a universe that knew me completely, through and through. I was in a state of anxiety, near panic, but from excitement at my new awareness rather than from fear. I was uneasy, agitated, high-strung and yet not uncomfortable.

I had slept in my car, in a parking lot. I felt the urge to get started, get moving, and go, though I had no destination. I began driving, made some wrong turns, and soon I was lost. This pleased me. Not knowing where I was sharpened my senses, kept my attention focused. Focus is essential to my survival.

I am not your upstanding citizen. Rather, I am a creature of the in-between, the cracks and crevices, the road less traveled, the alternative method, the other way, opposite of the recommended policy. I'm who your parents warned you about—a freethinker and free spirit. I have different ideas. I'm not the same. Some might call me a bad influence. I claim it's the only life I know, the way I evolved. I grew up in a house of drug addicts. A lot of their life and their sickness rubbed off on me, but in different ways. I learned how to get around the traditional, the conventional, accepted policies in life. I found out that there is another way, many other ways.

When I run out of money (as I have now) I have to live for free. Poverty is a wilderness that can be negotiated by wits. I live on coupons mostly. There are some on the floor of my car. They have served me well in the past.

I can't understand how people let themselves go hungry. I

have been broke, homeless, destitute, but never hungry for long. I feed myself by my wits. When you are truly hungry it isn't so hard to order a fine meal at a restaurant and simply accompany another party as they pay their check at the register and leave the restaurant. It is easy to open a package of cupcakes and stuff them whole in your mouth as you stand supposedly surveying items on a supermarket shelf. It is worthwhile to present useless, used, expired or fraudulent coupons to fast food employees and expect a free burger. They hear what you tell them and see what you want them to see. When you need them to, they honor the coupon, accept it without scrutiny, toss it in the drawer and hurry up your order because you told them it was coupon for a free burger. Why would they question you? (Although some have and many times I've been denied or had it pointed out to me that my scrap of colored paper was no good.) But just as many times I've been awarded my Luscious Burger, a thick greasy pad of meat on a bun, slobbered with sauce and manufactured paste and all things unnatural. I grew addicted to those slop-layered feasts in paper wrap. I grew addicted not just to the fat patty in pickle sauce and mayo gobs, but to the weight of the thing, like a brick in the paper bag they gave you. How could I even finish such a mass, I'd think, opening it up. I'd save some. But the more of it I swallowed, the more I wanted. In the end I knew I could have eaten two or three. My focus, my fixation was so strong that sometimes I circled back to the drive-thru to try again. I'd tell them at the speaker that I had a coupon for a free one. Then I'd pull up to the service window and hope the teenager or new immigrant would simply hand me the thing in a bag and forget to ask for the coupon. Sometimes they did, and I drove away smiling, contemplating my new brick of meat and its greasy aroma. Most times though they requested the coupon, the non-existent scrap of cutout paper that could feed me. Yet there was still a ruse or two. Hand them anything, an old dry cleaning receipt (yes, there was a time I had my clothes dry cleaned) or an advertisement from a newspaper. At times they took those! Or, I could glance around, search the car, pretend I had it a second ago and it must have slipped between the seats. If cars were behind me, waiting, the fast food server might say, "Okay, bring it next time," and hand me the treasured bag. It has happened.

I can tell the question formulating in your mind. If my focus is strong enough to feed me for free, why don't I set my sights on something bigger? Couldn't I just as easily focus on a big house, a new car, and wads of cash? But I thought I told you, one thing is as good as another. A cheeseburger is as good as a yacht. If my thinking wills me a free Luscious Burger, but not a Porsche, it doesn't mean I am a lower form of life. I am, instead, a clever manipulator of whatever items are available in my neighborhood of the universe. (Though perhaps I should move to a different corner of the cosmos, where I'll attract a different element. Attract is an intriguing, and also key concept. "Draw to you" or "let come to you," which is it? If I just sit still will that be enough? Surely, I'd attract something, someone, if I just sat still. Location would be important. I'd have to sit in a public place.)

But this day was not for sitting still. I continued making wrong turns for the entire afternoon. I discovered things that way that I never would have if I knew where I was going. Chance and happenstance are the elixir of life, especially the prescribed, homogenized sameness we're all bred to depend upon and cling to. In one new neighborhood I go into a church. I don't go to church when you do. I like empty churches on weekdays. I pretend someone is listening. Then I rest from the seeing. When I'm renewed I come out and stare closely at the variety of trees, note the houses and their yards, scan the multi-cultured faces. I experience, I learn, I am a visitor. These kinds of thoughts and notions are supposedly only for vacation times. We work extra hard to earn enough to send ourselves someplace where we can forget it all. But what is it we really need to forget? The time of day, the daily icons that define place, the rules of the road, the conventions and habits that lock us in. At the same time, we treasure these, especially if there's a threat they'll be taken away, or if we're placed in some of kind of dilemma or emergency. Lost in the forest, what you wouldn't give for a 7-Eleven, right? So you can walk in a 7-Eleven right now and thank God you don't have any crazy urge to explore wilderness. You can derive a sense of safety and peace of mind from that.

Remaining lost for the day put me at ease. Every time I saw a Luscious Burger palace I entered the drive-thru and attempted my trick. Four out of nine times I was rewarded with my toxic meal in a bag. But once I stalled at the window. The damn thing wouldn't start. Did the manager curse me; complain I was in the way? No! He came out and helped me push it aside. I sat where it stopped and ate. I had luck with Luscious Burgers.

But the car trouble upset me. I had moved up from riding the bus and I didn't want to go back. There were no attractive people on the bus and it bothered me to be among them. I'd looked over the lined faces and swearing lunatics and well dressed ugly women in jewelry and perfume until once I glanced up to see one looking at me. It was hard to accept belonging on the bus with them. But I did.

9.

The car saga continues getting worse. A tape has lodged inside the cassette player and will not come out. To hear the radio, even out of one speaker, I had to jam a pair of sunglasses in under the cassette. When I hit a bump in the road, the glasses shifted and the tape started. The droning half-speed music startled me, sounded like engine trouble. I frantically scanned dashboard gauges to see what was wrong. The singer's words were elongated moans. Sometimes I can't shut him off. Drivers stopped beside me at a light see me hunched, in a fit, my fingers snaked inside a slot, struggling.

I count on the rain to wash the car. But it hasn't rained in a while, so a crust has formed on the outside. This caked dirt hides the peeling paint in places. An interesting new pattern has formed on the hood. I stared at it so intently while waiting at a red light that I didn't realize all the horns were aimed at me. This pattern on my hood resembles a face, but only upside-down from the driver's point of view. I pulled over to the side to get out and study it from a different angle. Yes, it was a face, a face full of wrinkles. Closer, and after some time, I thought I recognized this face. This was undoubtedly the face of my landlady. Was the universe talking to me, telling me something? If so, it was nothing I didn't already know. She was after me still, even appearing now on the hood of my car. I purposely spit on her nose (it was only dirt on my hood). But it was so caked I couldn't scrape it away. I did manage to smear some of her nose down onto her mouth, but the effect was peculiar, unsettling. It made her face meaner, more intent on collecting the rent. I gave up and cursed the blue skies. I needed rain.

Miraculously, rain came that day. A gray blanket settled over us, like a layer of doom. It rained torrents.

The windshield wiper blade has split, one loose stringy piece of rubber flapping and twisting and wriggling with the back and forth movement of the blade, and now the crack is letting in tiny droplets that line up along the length of the windshield and drop off one by one at the end, forming an ever-growing splotch on the floor. It's of no help that I have a hole in my shoe under the big toe. It requires that I position my foot differently now as I drive. That may not sound like any big deal. But it changes everything. Once I shift my foot, I must angle my body slightly to one side. That affects my steering posture and cramps my gear-shifting arm. Adjusting to that, my vision of the road is impaired at least twenty percent on the right-hand side. In the meantime, the splotch broadens. I am being forced nearly out of my seat in an effort to keep dry. Already my foot has slipped unconsciously back to its original spot several times and my sock is soaked through in the front. You see what a drop of water can do? It can change the course of a life.

10.

I am an ant. There's no denying it. I go this way and that, with a reason, without. I stop and go, stop and go, wander about. I change directions suddenly, only to go back the way I came again. It's all very serious, meaningful, vital, and all for nothing. I know it's for nothing and yet I continue to dart her and there, often in a hurry, and causing myself discomfort and hardship, weariness and fatigue. I place great importance upon my doings and then laugh at them; they're ridiculous. But what else is there for me? If I sat calmly instead would it make any difference? Sit, get up, wait, move, remain still, never pause, am I any more or less because of one or the other? I suppose I do what I must. Perhaps my only mistake is to ever think about it at all. Maybe the only thing that matters is whether I am happy as an ant. If I am a happy ant, then I scramble around without direction, to no particular destination happily. It is enough to be an ant, and probably only a dysfunction to question my ant life. But then, I am a dysfunctional ant who wonders what being an ant really means, when we all know that it means nothing. And even though it means nothing, we must all be serious ants on the way to nowhere very determinedly. In fact, it is desirable to be a better ant than the other ants you come across, if there is anything to being an ant at all. The perfect ant is the quest. Or, perhaps it is best to dream of being a supreme ant one day after you are a dead ant. That is the most an ant can hope for. In the meantime, what a serious ant I am supposed to be—a little progress here, a little progress there, but really, nowhere much in the end. I suppose I should find another ant, but I have before and it's always the same result. We meet, exchange our ant fluids and knowledge, and then in an ant moment, we are gone from each other. Of course, we do circle back for another round occasionally. Or we keep going into another crevice of the ant journey and never know our fellow ant's fate. Even when two ants do settle down they continue to scurry about, and it's still the same ant game. Deep down ants know that all other ants are extremely expendable, except for the ants that they know. If ants are washed down a bathroom sink drain in another house it's too bad but that's ant life and death. But if an ant friend succumbs to spray or wanders into an ant trap never to return it is the worst of all possible ant fates. That is what being a serious ant is all about. Dart here, dart there, worry, get crushed or drowned. In the meantime it is best not to think of it at all, and to win trophies for ant accomplishments.

Ants are strong, noble creatures. They pick up their injured ant buddies and carry them, though God knows where. Solitary ants start this way and that and go around and around, seemingly never getting anywhere. But even ants carrying wounded ants do the same thing, apparently getting nowhere with a heavier burden. Perhaps there is an ant trophy to be had somewhere for shouldering this extra burden.

11.

I am parked at a mall, in the furthest spot from the entrance. No one uses these spots. They don't like to walk the extra fifty feet. They will drive around and around the spots closest to the mall doors, waiting for someone to leave, rather than park easily in an empty spot a few feet further away. Even now I see them circling, ignoring the rows of spots near me. They could have parked where I am, gone inside, and done half their shopping already. They'll walk and walk in the mall, all day long. But they will not walk in the parking lot. That's all right with me. I purposely parked outside the lines, partially into the next space, claiming a little extra territory for the moment. I might get out and stretch, or lean against my car and stare up at the great good sky.

I have not been shopping for some time. Shopping makes people happy. At least until they get home and try their new item and it isn't as good as they thought, or they use it for a while with complete satisfaction and then it breaks. Then there are phone calls to customer service, and appointments to fix it, and repair charges, and general aggravation. That is the nature of our consumer society. We hate to work. We hate our lousy jobs, those who do work, I mean, and I'll admit I'm not one of you. So you trudge to the factory or the warehouse or the office in the morning and set yourself down and pump quarts of coffee into your blood and rev it up and go go go until the end of the day, trying not to think about what you're doing, hating every minute of your repetitive motion that adds a spring to a toaster, or attaches a switch to a toy truck so it can sound a fire alarm, or you nail a leg of wood to a cheap couch or you slap processed baloney onto starchy bread for a kid's lunch, or stare, stare, at a computer screen, or. . . .you know what I mean, it's what you all do every day.

But what do you do with your free time and nights and weekends? Most of you rush to the store, where other workers are hating their eight to twelve hours, and push and shove and get in line to buy the item that unhappy workers resented getting out of bed at dawn to make for you. There you have it, a country full of unhappy workers laboring slap-dash and unconcerned to produce an inferior product, all to earn a wage so that they themselves can take that wage and go out and buy the totally inferior product haphazardly assembled by another unhappy worker. We produce crap to earn a wage to buy crap. No one is applying craftsmanship and superior skills to their product. Everyone only wants to rush through their required task to get home and read advertisements for what's on sale and plan to go buy it. It's absurd! What are they buying? Crap that others have rushed to complete so that they can get home on time. Then it all breaks or doesn't work right and you complain and wonder why. There's no mystery. No one gets real satisfaction out of doing the job. How could they, when their job is to assemble crap? Then everyone tries to get real satisfaction out of assembled crap. How could they when it was not produced to provide satisfaction, but to meet a five o'clock deadline so that the worker could say, "Done!" and hurry home.

I, however, am happy with crap. I have learned to love crap. I can pay little or nothing for an item and then expect it to malfunction or break down because I knew all along it was defective in the most intrinsic sense, that is, nothing went into it, no love, no care, no skill, no workmanship, perhaps what went into it was resentment and even spite. In fact, I have learned to seek out the most defective items—shirts with upside down pockets, groceries with misprinted package labels, etc., etc. They cost less and provide the same defective experience as supposedly correctly manufactured goods.

I enjoy cheap things. Most people enjoy the finer things and deplore or just tolerate cheap things. But to me, cheap things are just as useful as expensive ones. Take a bed for instance. I gazed in a store window at the most luxurious, lush, soft, satiny, pillow

covered king size imaginable. The kind you sink into in a form
fitting way that surrounds your flesh and nearly caresses you with
softness. That truly is a desirable bed, I thought. But I get a deep,
sound, full night's sleep on a fifteen-dollar mattress on the floor
when I am tired. It's when I'm awake and desiring sleep that the
appeal of the luxury bed is keen. But that doesn't translate to the
actual act of sleeping. A luxury bed is actually for the time you're
awake in bed. Some very deep sleeps I've had on beach sand, grass,
or a hammock. So long as I'm thoroughly stretched out and the
sleeping surface is not hard, the best of sleeps occurs. A cheap
mattress accomplishes this, and even upon waking on it, is normally
comfortable enough to lounge on. And upon waking from a
thorough, restful slumber of nine or ten hours, I have never missed
that luxury bed, nor even thought of it.

The same goes for a car. Yes, of course, we all want to ride in
comfort. But the point of a car is to get you somewhere. Though I
have never had a luxury car, I have always gotten where I am going
(until now, that is, as I've finally realized there's nowhere to go). I
am not speaking of a running car versus one that breaks down, but
of a car equipped with all the latest and the best to supply the
equivalent of happiness on a chassis, as opposed to the mere chassis
itself with enough surrounding metal to separate you from the
road. I like the idea of a "loaded" vehicle of the highest class available
to me when I choose to travel. But when I do travel, I go from one
place to another whether it's in a luxury car or a cheap one. Cheap
cars have taken me across the continent, around a state, and down
the block and back. I have gone that far in cheap cars. When I got
to my destination, I don't recall missing the loaded luxury vehicle
that would have done the same thing for me, gotten me from one
place to another. Instead, what I recall is the exhilaration of having
completed the journey without breaking down.

So, in fact it is always the "idea" of something better, more
luxurious and expensive that makes the difference in the basic
services that things like beds and cars deliver. The supposedly
"better" product is always desirable, and admittedly, would be my

choice also if I had a choice. But the cheap item at least delivers the basic result—sleep, or distance covered, etc.—once the product is used. That is why I can appreciate cheap items when others demean them. If they work at all they've exceeded expectations.

When we are done producing cheap items at our jobs that we hate so much, or even while still working at them, we fawn over advertisements for island getaways, tropical retreats, six days and seven nights of sun and sand and surf, pina coladas, bikinis and sunsets, and the ocean breeze. The lure of the vacation is the idea that we'll actually be the characters in TV commercials and brochures when we get there. We'll be the one-dimensional, smiling, carefree cardboard snorkeler, or the bright-eyed blank reeling in the trophy fish, or the star-crossed romantic seated in front of a picture-perfect steak and lobster. Instead, we arrive only to find ourselves. It is still us, you are still you, still the guy with the peptic ulcer whose wife drinks too much, still the unlucky schlub whose battery died near the White Oak exit, still the overweight woman from New Jersey who wishes she were a novelist. You find you cannot escape into the identity (or lack of) of the sales pitch. Most events and activities are like that. Plans are made for the concert, the show, the big event, main attraction, etc., etc. (There's always one brewing, always a big day on the way.) But when the time arrives, it's still just a day, or a night. Despite the layers of new clothing and carefully coordinated accessories, you are still you. No matter who the act is you go to see, no matter how big, how acclaimed, it is just you again, sitting in a seat now, watching, listening (perhaps daydreaming, but what a waste of an expensive ticket!) or probably you are looking around to see who sees you.

Sadly, you did not become the pictured advertisement, devoid of your own thoughts, cares, concerns and troubles that tempted you to attend. That is the huge disappointment of illusion. The someplace where your past dissolves, the promised land where glee is your only emotion, the sought-after destination that will transform you from yourself into the media image of a more perfect you is never to be found. It can only be imagined, and you will pay anything, everything, to have it. Sorry, it is not for sale. You buy, however, the bait and switch tactic. Here it is. Here is what you get, says the salesman. All you ever wanted. Your dream you. So you travel ten thousand miles and arrive in your own company and must put up with yourself, only now a bit poorer. Sure, you get the lush room, pool, and all the amenities. You get entertainment, boat rides, dancing. What you don't get is the transformation into the cherished caricature of you. Your warts are still attached. Sorry, no refunds. Wherever you go, there you are. Perhaps some day it may occur to you—if you need a change of scenery, it can be engineered from the inside.

12.

This system is not serving me well. I have decided on a new system, a more direct form of communicating my needs and getting them fulfilled by the universe in general. I am now speaking aloud to the universe every day. I have no companion, not even the gnat anymore, and if you spotted me on the sidewalk you'd think I was one of those nut cases who'd lost his shopping cart, because I carry on a conversation with someone who is apparently not there. But it is not someone with whom I am speaking, it is the "One", the larger entity, the bigger picture in which I am a dot. I speak and it listens, and then it talks back to me, in events, occurrences, coincidences, and daily encounters with other dots. We have a very intimate but one-sided relationship because it knows everything about me and I seem to know only a very little about it. The saving grace is that it seems to want to tell me all about itself, if I would only listen. But listening is not so easy because it means attuning the sixth sense. I must be vigilant, alert to clues, hints, omens, signs and symbols that will lead me to what's best for me. Apparently, they're everywhere, all the time, right in front of my eyes. But I can't always see them.

That's what I meant when I stated at the beginning that seeing precisely what is visible is important to me. I must see, not only the real thing itself, but also the realer reality it communicates. That's the way to connect the dots. It's all right in front of me. But as I said, I'm also a dot in it.

13.

My car has finally coughed its last exhaust and I am walking. Walking is not so bad. I have become intimate with neighborhoods now. I know the cracks in the sidewalks, the best smelling bakeries, the newsstands to linger at, the alleys and back streets. I walk for miles and miles, past so many storefronts and never go in one. I pass the beautiful houses with their landscaped yards and double garages, sometimes sidestepping sprinklers; other times letting them hit me. I don't budge as barking dogs rush at me, don't lift my head as cars let me pass, but sometimes smile at old yard workers watering their grass. I have nowhere to go and no time to be there so I don't mind walking. I am in no hurry. My only concern is what to do with that dead chassis of mine that sits on a city block. I suppose I could let them just haul it away. I should feel happy. My troubles will simply be hooked up to a truck and towed to a heap and dumped there. So I am left with just my two feet, so what. Look at how the rest of my concerns disappear. I don't need to fix it, or worry about its appearance, or sweat tickets, or buy gas, or do the registration paperwork, or supply insurance. I won't worry about accidents. I am free of it.

But the way it died nearly killed me, and then when I lived through it I nearly died of mortification. You see, I was on a busy street when the puttering thing lurched and growled, telling me it didn't want to keep going, but I made it, my foot forcing the accelerator down, pumping, like I might break through the floorboard and kick the engine itself into continuing. "You can't stop!" I cried. "I just put a dollar's worth of gas in you!" I was determined to get all of my money's worth. But the rolling scab wrestled me, belching smoke, jerking unhappily. Drivers rolling by stared at me, made faces, laughed. I pounded on my steering wheel and rode the stuttering motion of my car like a loping horse. I would have whipped it if I could. "Go! Go!" I ordered it, aware of horns sounding and threats hurled from shiny late models piled up behind me.

"Get off the road!"

"Move it or park it!"

I should have given every one of them the finger, held it high and pointed it one after another as they honked and bitched. But instead I smiled and shrugged, apologetic, as if I didn't know what was wrong, as if betrayed by my four-wheeled friend. It was not my fault. I tried to communicate with a helpless expression. It was the maker, the factory, or the incompetent assembly line that had put the damn thing together. Or I had bought the wrong gas, something low-grade that should not have been allowed in this country. I tried to communicate that with my face. But drivers frowned and glared and wouldn't understand, giving me the finger, looking as if they'd shoot me next. Though I'm sure most had guns, none had time, swerving around me, roaring forward to beat the clock.

Then it happened, the rattling package of loose nuts and bolts shook beneath me, convulsed around me, let go a mechanical moan and died there in the street. It was not a bloodless end. It did leave its mark. I had to get out amidst the jeers and obscenities of screeching lane changers and saw fluids dripping, oil blotting the asphalt. What could I do but stare, helpless? I found out right away.

"Push it, asshole!" they shouted.

"Get it outta the way!"

Vicious faces behind windshields pinned me with their eyes. I had no insurance, no one to call, no money for repair, and no recourse. I rolled my sleeves and bent behind my hulk, applied my shoulder. It resisted, inched forward, a burden to the end. I pushed hard and my wreck gained momentum. Veering cars dodged as I angled to the curb, but no spot was vacant. It rolled toward parked cars. At first I dug my heels in the street and tried to stop it. The impact was minimal, really.

I didn't stick around to see how bad the scratch was. They could have the thing. It was worth at least what it would cost to repaint a fender. I was donating it, offering it as payment, in advance. The back seat was still in excellent condition. No one had ever sat in it. I had few passengers (okay, none), and I hadn't even thrown much back there, just newspapers and fast food containers. Yes, the back seat alone was worth the price of fixing a dent. Anyone could remove it, easily. They could put it in their own car, if they needed a new back seat. I left the scene with a clear conscience. For a moment I even felt I'd given myself a raw deal. That back seat loomed in my mind as more valuable than I'd given it credit for. I thought of returning for it. I could have gotten face value for it at a dealer. But it would be tough carrying a back seat. All right then, they could have it. The tires I admit were bald, and there were no other good parts. The sunglasses were still usable, though it would take a pair of pliers to dislodge them from the tape player. But no one could tell me the back seat wouldn't compensate for what had happened. I did the only thing I could. In my mind, I let go of the back seat, forgot about it. There would be other back seats, and perhaps, other cars.

14.

I am one moment from a complete blow up. If I don't end myself, I will fall apart spontaneously at some point. I'll scream and convulse, drip spittle out of me. That's the emotional blank of my soul. I want to feel and have no one to feel with. Any feelings I have are a waste. I'm about to self-destruct. I swear it. (I am using this as a ruse, a tool. I have to do something to manipulate my circumstances. Perhaps if I threaten to end it all I'll get a break of some sort. You see, I know the universe is listening. I know it hears me.) I'm threatening to walk out on . . . everything. It's come down to a simple yes or no. Pay rent or quit. Funny how that option is always available, at your fingertips, under your control, while all else is an unfathomable maze no one has the map to. I can't seem to get to the corner store for milk today, just somehow can't make it—you know the feeling, right? But I can vaporize myself, and my home, and three more houses on the block, and the corner store, too, just by striking a match to the fuse of the lethal weapons cache I keep collected in the basement. (I exaggerate. We know I have no basement, no weapons, no house, not even a match.) No, in my own specific case I'd need a knife to slash my wrists. That's a standard image, the way it's done. Presently all I can lay my hands on is a plastic version. That would take some effort, sawing and carving. I'd have to whittle myself to death. The alternative: throw myself off a high building. That's what high buildings are good for—another standard way to go. Or jump in front of a train. Even cross against the light, though there's a chance you'd end up paralyzed from the neck down instead. What good would that be? One strange aspect of suicide (yes, that's what we're talking about here) is its deep-rooted connection to masturbation. Might as well do one as the other. Each is a concession to the world at large that you're no longer part of it. Left to your own devices—by your own hand. Self-flagellation I've heard it called, by religious people. Self-pleasure it's called by others; also religious people. But then, suicide, to the perpetrator, must be a form of self-pleasure. Perhaps it's the ultimate in self-pleasure. Maybe masturbating yourself to death is the ideal.

Yes, I'm on the verge. At least, in death, I should have company. After all, the dead outnumber us. Once dead, you join the many hundreds of billions, trillions of billions of dead. Surely there's no loneliness there . . . so many of them . . .

In the meantime, I'm alone and it won't cooperate with me. It won't let me have a friend or a companion to experience the miracle of all creation with. I can't behold the true magnificence of a mountain or the sea because I can't reflect it anywhere, into another's eyes. It evaporates with me, into nothing, nada. The mountain isn't so great. In fact, it's in the way. The sea is a dismal flat bore. Who thinks they're so astounding, momentous? They only are when another soul is present to agree. And really, it's probably just two people satisfied not to be alone that makes myth out of boulders and deep water.

What I want is another; then all things will be miracles. But without another, I am left with it as my only friend. And it holds me prisoner. It has me at its mercy. I am its slave, its individual eye, just for seeing itself. It won't let me in, just has me watch; makes me watch. I can't participate. At first I try to work with it, knowing it's all around and all encompassing. I just say, "Take me, I'll go with your flow." No fighting, the path of least resistance. But it doesn't take me anywhere, like I'm in the soup but not getting stirred. So I become active and try to prompt it but the result is the same. No entry for me, no connection, I am alone. I get defiant and blast it as illegitimate. The whole universe is not interconnected. I'm not a cog in the big wheel. I'm not unfolding as it unfolds. People and things everywhere are not all part of one grand design. There is no deeper level of being even if you look closely and pay constant vigilance. Portents and signs and omens do not exist in front of your eyes and ears at every moment. Really, this whole place, the whole face of this earth is no more than exactly what it appears to be. Soul and spirit and God are all beyond my reach, navigable only after life and only by having been good now and followed the Ten Commandments and confessed to sins. At about that point I begin to laugh. I begin to feel my unique connection, start to understand once again, and I feel. I do not feel alone. I know that it is with me.

It is me. And I am it. I understand that this creature is more than I know, more than I could know, much more intricate and complex than I could imagine, stranger, more bizarre than I could pretend. It is not what I thought it was. It is a mind, a vast, ethereal mind, and solid as matter wherever I touch. Its terrain is also different than I'd perceived. The true terrain is mental and the currency is consciousness. I go where I think. I have thought myself into a corner where I am watching it and it is being me.

15.

Today I have decided to add myself to the story of life, as a comma. I am at least that, at least a comma. If I am not enough of an entity to constitute a word, I am still a speed bump between ideas. Have I told you yet that I am an incredibly lonely man named Flex Ponderosa? I have no friends and no family in my vicinity (though I do have a sordid and stuporous drug-addicted family far from here). There is no explaining me; I am so devoid of normalcy. I can't get out of this head I'm in, so don't suggest treatment. There is no treatment better than reality anyway.

My reality at the moment consists of watching my dust ball. True, it's no longer just a speck. It has grown, accumulated weight. It is not quite a puff, but certainly on its way. Its contents have become a bit more solid. Something has arisen out of nothing.

Watching is such an accepted behavior it's never expressed as simply sitting with your eyes open. Paying big bucks for a sports event (where you're herded like cattle to your narrow seat and held captive for hot dogs and peanuts six times their normal price) is seen as an activity. Actually, you just sit. Entire weekends passed this way are considered worthy. In this world, when you watch, you do. Stare at a tube (not another person, but an electronic tube) and you've done something. Take a long drive. Forget that all you've done was sit and stared. Think of the vistas you've passed, the sights you've seen. Bird watching is considered a worthy pursuit. You may even take notes. Yes, watching is big, big . . . unless you are watching nothing. By that, I mean appearing to be watching nothing, for that is what contemplating this life, world, universe and the true big picture looks like. It looks like you're doing nothing. And, that is not only disallowed, it is unforgivable. You must actually be watching "something" not just everything. Staring at life as it unfolds, fixing the moment in your mind's eye, with your real eye on nothing in particular, doesn't cut it. You're labeled suspicious, or out of it, while all about you the knowing, intelligent beings of the universe sit slumped or straight backed and gape at football games and sitcoms and bikini contests. Action must pass before your eyes for your watching to be deemed worthy, that is, action where something obviously happens—a man is kicked in the head by a spinning martial artist, or a ball is batted over a fence. If you suddenly (or even gradually, however you arrive at the point) understand that everything is a miracle, an inexplicable, inexpressible whopper of a miracle, and that the workings of this monstrous and beautiful place—or organism, I don't know which— are profoundly subtle and entertaining, and that there's much undiscovered right in front of your eyes, discoveries available at any time and easily accessible and highly unpredictable (which is the fun of this miracle), then you are truly observing. It is only when your focus shifts from the man with the ball to the immense grandeur of the alive universe that watching is truly observing. I'm just sitting here watching the wheels, went one ditty, composed by a pop hero who dropped out. If a pop hero opts to give it all up, recline and gaze at the omnipresent miracle, what then are the rest of us striving for?

Watching, observing my dust ball, seeing it move, I realized I had formed a thought. It was a thought or else it was dust. It concerned the furthest reaches of the universe itself. But when I say the furthest reaches, I mean something entirely different than what you might think. This is what I thought.

I thought about the space program. We may as well just shoot money into space. Put fifty million in a cannon and blow it out our atmosphere! Outer space is a money burner. We already know we can go light years without finding anything alive. When we do discover something, it's likely to be a Welfare Planet, very in need of our help. We'll finance a generation of space rescuers and send them off to give aid, and probably never see them again. I might be the first to volunteer. Can you imagine that? I would be famous, as the first man to volunteer to travel light years away to help a starving, sick planet in need. I would receive a huge sendoff. Everyone on Earth would know who I was. My picture would be broadcast worldwide, waving goodbye. That would be a moment, the moment we all dream about, the big time. Then I would be gone and never get to enjoy one second of fame. I would be off the planet on my way to a humanitarian mission. I would leave behind all the millions who had heard of me and never celebrate myself. No dinners, no limos, no pretty girls, no parties, no sleeping late, no drugged-out bliss, no celebrity status, just lonesome dark space until I reached the crying helpless of the desperate planet and then nothing but hard work. Earth would probably never see me again, except in satellite transmissions where my picture would appear and the average person on the street could glance up for a moment and say to his wife, "Oh look, it's what's his name, the guy who went off into outer space to help that dying civilization. You remember him, don't ya, honey?" And she'd say, "Oh yeah, is he back? Is there going to be a parade?" But I'd probably never come back, having traveled so far and there being so much to do for the unfortunates at the other end of the galaxy. I'd be like a historical figure, someone already dead but important in a certain context, an answer in a crossword puzzle. There would be news reports about my progress and maybe by then some kind of intergalactic e-mail so I could respond to fans. But it wouldn't be like fame on Earth. In fact, it would be the stupidest alternative, fame on Earth while you're on another planet and can't enjoy one second of it. Fame on Earth precisely because you left Earth and probably won't make it back—at least, not until after death. I'd live the whole rest of my famous life in the most remote obscurity possible, barely subsisting on rationed supplies as I help the unfortunates of the Welfare Planet, living with them, as one of them, like some sort of cosmic Mother Teresa, unable to parlay any of it into a larger house or a big-screen TV or any of the modern comforts or amenities such as my own horse stable, or a bowling alley built into my den or three swimming pools in the shape of antique cars. But then I'd die, and they'd ship my body back across the universe, a casket through space, and my remains would enjoy a hero's return to the elderly who remembered me, and a curious notice from youth who'd never heard of me. There might be a parade. Or, my remains might be scorned, by political activists who opposed sending our resources to help the Welfare Planet. My coffin would be spit upon by the poor here who wondered why I had to siphon food and sustenance away from them to aid a race of aliens, and I would be infamous, a symbol of all that's wrong in the world and they'd dispose of me in an unmarked grave. Such is the contents of my dust ball.

16.

I recall now that I am on a mission, but it has not gone well. It must be going terribly, in fact, for I'd forgotten I even was on a mission. But, yes, I do have a purpose, even more difficult than venturing light years to help the poor. I'm supposed to save a family. That's it. How could I have forgotten? These are people I know and love, blood relations. How could they slip my mind? They are a family of drug addicts, that's how they've slipped my mind. They are useless and hopeless, deformed and demented, and I can only picture them as lumps now, though I'm certain that some time ago, I don't know how long, they were beautiful and important. Now they have no teeth, their skin is scarred, they're listless and overweight and their minds are gone. But once they were pure and remarkably human, as perfectly formed and precious as newborns. Once they were loving and witty and intelligent and had dreams of a future, dreams of fame even, as I do. Once they mattered. I was with them in those days, days of fresh youth and excitement about what would come of us in this world. Then gradually they began to change, a little bit at a time. As I've said, despair is an incremental thing. It does not come upon one suddenly, or from out of the blue like catastrophe. That day is not sunny and bright one moment and cloudy the next. Those clouds form far out on the horizon and drift ever so slowly into view, into consciousness as it were, until vision becomes a cloud, quite naturally, and a cloud becomes what one expects to see each time the eyes are opened. Despair thickens as wisps of a cloud. It grows dense, until it can't be seen through, can't be penetrated. Catastrophe is a storm that rolls in unannounced and thunders and plunders, strewing its carnage and wreckage where all can see and setting exact terms for the cleanup. Despair just surrounds one like a creeping fog until you've lost your bearings and don't know how to get back. There's no cleanup involved, because you can't espy the mess. The mess is in your head. That's where their mess formed, the family I am supposed to save. They messed up inside their heads. You see, they did not believe in their own dreams. They did not have faith. They sought an easy way out of this condition we're all in. They saw that life, for them, would be a struggle. They had nothing in life. They were much like the unfortunates on the Welfare Planet. They were born to poverty and need, and deserted by their parents, left to figure it out and fend for themselves. They did not perceive the great big miracle surrounding them as I do. They did not understand the cosmic joy that permeates daily life, even in the silences. They did not see the phenomenon of existence as sacred. They saw only struggle and deprivation and growing despair. They did not grow their hope. Hope is a beacon that cuts through the fog of despair but it, too, is incremental. Hope needs focus and nurturing. It starts as a thin line of light and expands into a glowing rapture only after much belief and concentration. It is not like joy that overcomes one with wondrous good feeling all at once. Hope is a small, spreading smile that widens, widens, until that smile is the face of the world. Joy is sudden sharp laughter that propels you out of your seat. They gave up hope but remained expectant of joy. They thought one hope should lead to joy, that one hope was enough. They did not think that hope was of itself an asset, a sustainer. So soon they had no hope. Without hope they gave way to despair, gradually, a little bit at a time. Despair worked for them much as hope would have if they'd let it. They grew their despair and now they are monsters, distorted pictures of who they used to be.

But I am sick of discussing them. That is why I have forgotten them. They are ugly creatures of the lowest depths. Their hair is matted and caked with dust. They lie inert and soil their own beds. They clean nothing and no longer even recognize dirt as dirt. They inhabit a netherworld of narcotic unreality.

My own despair closes in unless I contemplate the expansive optimism of my new name. If you see me on the street call me Ponder, like Howdy, Ponder. I will no doubt be on my way to a job interview, or looking for a place to live. I will be doing normal things, with little success. You are no less sacred and holy than I am. You are no less metaphysical and psychic than me. You are no less a spiritual and emotional orb of light glowing in the eternal abyss than I. Why then don't you seem to know it, or act it? How do you take so seriously your job and the errands you must run? Why can't I put on that kind of face? Why am I, I alone almost, one in a sea of so many, struck with, plagued with this unrelenting truth?

17.

I have seen too much, that is true. I have seen beyond, seen even more than I want to see. Yes, I have seen through this "life" and its absurdities. I understand now that I am a tube, that's all, a tube. I put food (if you can call what I eat food) and other substances in me, only to have them pop out of me at the other end. Constantly, over and over, in one end and out the other, all to maintain this tube. I am a pipe, with a stream running in and fluids dripping out. Base, basic, as simple and crude as can be, I am a tube. We are all tubes. Yet we aspire to such grace, such holiness. We are tubes and potential angels at the same time. We are tubes that say prayers—how comical—and tubes that make wishes, and tubes that believe in salvation. What is salvation for a tube, to no longer be a tube? To be an ethereal, body-less wisp of pureness floating above the dirt and the infection and the never-ending processing of raw material through our tube selves? That is what tubes think. Yes, tubes do think. They don't have to think, and many of them do not think at all, just process process process, in-out, in-out, and that may be smarter than actually thinking. What does thinking get a tube? If it starts thinking about its tube-ness, thinking will most likely make a tube self-conscious. Yes, that is a good one, a self-conscious tube. There are so many of them. They think and they think, and they think they are more than just a tube. They think they're above being a tube. They do not want to deal with the other end of their tube, but they have to. They do not want to accept that they are creatures of dirt and waste. They try to hide that part. But that cannot keep them from surrendering to the contortions and excretions of the body. When the body calls they run. They cannot control themselves. They are forced to face facts, that they are tubes. They are foul, smelly tubes. One day they will rot right back into the soil. But don't think about it. Pretend you are a princely thing, a creature of wonder and meaning. Give yourself an identity and create a heaven where your higher self can find peace after life as a tube. Then being a tube isn't so bad. There's a payoff. Be a good tube. Put only the correct, pure elements of life into your tube. Love your tube, esteem your tube, and bless your tube. Don't hurt any other tubes. Recycle.

But perhaps the universe is a tube and you are the raw material being recycled for eternity. You are now in the bowels of the universe. Soon you will come out the other end—that is death. In the meantime, you journey through the darkness of the intestines—that is life—tubes within tubes, the whole thing one long process. It doesn't seem sacred or holy or Catholic or Muslim. It seems scary. Like this place is one large organic being eating itself, chewing itself, swallowing itself, digesting itself and excreting itself to be eaten again. Somewhere among its foodstuff are the tubes, us, who believe. Ha ha, tubes who believe. Yes, in the great eternal intestines we have created something to believe in, a class higher than tubes. Yet, the whole thing is a tube. Okay, we're entitled to our fantasies as tubes. As thinking tubes we get to pretend that we're not in one larger tube that recycles us just as we recycle meat loaf.

But we are missing the point! The recycling of meat loaf is holy! It's sacred! The dirt is pure! Thinking tubes that believe in an afterlife as something other than tubes are the holiest, most sacred things. We deny our nature and aspire to a hypothetical perfection—absent our tube-ness—when indeed we are already created in the image of perfection. To be a tube is to be perfect.

18.

Let me tell you how I fit in. I know I have intimated, if I have not said outright, that I am a misfit. I do not conform to the usual patterns and standards, and I do not meet expectations, and I am generally considered a defect of some sort in our pleasant everyday lives. If I would just shut up and get a job and keep my nose busy I wouldn't have time to walk around dreaming up ridiculous notions about what it all means and what we're doing here. But I'm a stubborn misfit and an outspoken one. I happen to feel that there is a place for me after all, as a reflector of all of you, as a philosopher of sorts, as the symbol for what everyone despises—the man with free time to wonder.

But, as a man, as one guy (one big guy I'll have you remember; you do recall my name, don't you) I am connected to you and to all things, just as you are. So what? So what, you say. So I'm connected, so big deal. Why don't I use some of my connections to earn a living? I'm not that well connected. Isn't that funny? I am intimately connected to you and to all things—the earth and sky, the animals, the grass and flowers, the cement of sidewalks and the materials of houses and buildings, everything really—yet I can't make a worthwhile connection in the land of employment. Well, we'll get back to that. The point is that I am one responsible person. I am responsible for one person's worth of reality. Have you noticed how closely the word reality resembles realty? That's right, I'm a bit of the universe's real estate. As a piece of real estate in the universe, I am part of a community. As part of that community, I must do my share. Well, realistically, everybody does his share. You cannot help but do your share if you're here at all. Every move you make, every step you take (to cite a once popular song) is part of doing your share in the universe. You can't help it. You are connected. You are connected even to me, no matter if that fact fills you with distaste. To reference an old, old, very old analogy, you are a ripple in the pond, as I am, and all are. The pebble was thrown long ago. Don't ask me who threw it; we are getting to that. But, as one person's worth of reality, my actions influence your actions. Even if you are in China or on the moon or across the universe (to cite another pop song) what I do influences you and everyone else. It works vice versa as well, with what you do touching and influencing me. Now, I'm not blaming you or anyone for my condition or my state. After all, I can't tell which one of you has acted in a manner that may have caused me to starve or go mad. I can't pinpoint the source. That's part of my philosophy—no one can discern the source to life and all its odd characteristics. No one can connect the dots. (Philosophy, by the way, anyone's—or mine's—is not meant as an attempt to figure it all out, but as an approach to existing and a way to make it work.)

However, if you or I act irresponsibly, it will not help the rest of us. If you or I act responsibly, on the other hand, it will help the rest of us. It's that simple. Act responsibly. Help the rest get along. They are all just as baffled at being here as you are; though some think they have it all figured out. I'll compare it to traffic to make my point. Drive responsibly. That sounds simple enough, doesn't it? Don't weave or speed or make reckless moves. Don't endanger others. I'm not trying to take the fun out of life. Don't accuse me of that. Take a joyride in the country, peel out and burn rubber, gun the engine once in a while. For god's sake, live! But contribute as well. When I say exist responsibly I mean so that all things function a bit more smoothly due to your attitude and your actions. The same for driving; drive with all of traffic in mind. Then drive for the good of all traffic. Not just for yourself to get where you're going as fast as possible, but for everyone to arrive at their destinations safely and smoothly. Preachy, do I sound preachy? I'm not telling you how to drive. I don't even drive myself anymore, so it would be awfully presumptuous for me to tell you how to drive. But when I drove I tried to do so with the good of all traffic in mind. I would slow to allow another driver to change lanes, especially in a difficult, crowded flow. I would adjust my speed to facilitate the easiest, most fluid flow of cars together. Now do you get it, do you see what I mean? I would treat every car as an equal, entitled to its share of the road, and maneuver so that all cars got where they were going with as little trouble as possible. That's what I mean about being responsible.

Being a person means the same thing—live so that all other beings can live as comfortably and even joyously as possible. In my small way I try to serve the greater good of all humanity. Do you understand my nature a bit better now? Do you see how my name illustrates my essence? Do you comprehend where I get a sense of importance, even grandeur simply by being alive? Does that explain why I don't need to buy every new object on the market as soon as it appears, and why I don't focus my human attention on new clothes and perfect curtains? Am I just a smidgeon clearer to you now? I hope so. I do. But don't get me wrong. I don't mean to imply that everybody should think the way I do. No, that's impossible, even though it's a standard expectation in our world— that everybody must think the same and act the same.

19.

I am a man of many theories. I'll tell you about my Everybody Theory, and I will expose the world of mortal souls as a bunch of mental midgets. Now, if you do something irregular yet harmless in your car, such as double-park, some bright soul will stop you and point and say, "What if everybody did that?" (I'm not bringing this up because it happened to me a short while ago, and because I grew upset and shouted profanities at the idiot who told me to move. There's a larger purpose here, you'll see.)

In the course of life, if you sidestep the rules and regulations— once again in a minor, harmless fashion that hurts no one but allows a little convenience for you—that same type of person will jump up and say, "What if everybody did that?" Well, I have news for you. Beyond the forces of nature that act upon our tubes and make us eat, breathe, sleep and go to the bathroom, there is nothing that everybody does. Behavior-wise, and thought-wise, for one, we cannot get everybody to do the same thing even when we try. We cannot get everyone to vote the same (for those who do vote; I have never voted and I advocate it for all. It's the same thing, isn't it, trying to get everyone to vote, or trying to get them all to stop. In either case, it's trying to get everybody to do the same thing, and that's impossible.). We cannot get everyone to agree how tax money should be spent. We cannot get everybody to drive carefully—and these are things we try to get everybody to do the same. Most importantly, we cannot get everybody to agree on what God is. Obviously, the nature of our existence here is to be disparate, at odds, pro and con, for and against, black and white, on and on and on. So, it is actually acceptable to break out of the mold at times, in small ways that perhaps offer one an insignificant (except to that one) advantage for a moment in this struggle. That is my Everybody Theory—that basically, there's nothing that everybody agrees on. I use it to allow myself small deviations from the larger code and order of things. I don't want to be reprimanded or dissed because of it. If I scrape together enough change to order a plain hamburger from one of those happy-faced fast-food chain restaurants (no, they are not restaurants, they are mini amusement parks with a grill) and, upon collecting my order, the worker accidentally hands me the wrong bag, a thick heavy bag I know is not mine, full of juicy gobs of crap that might kill me in sufficient doses but tastes real good, then it's okay to take it, and walk away without a word, knowing perfectly well it isn't mine. It's a small mistake that I accept as a kindness from the universe at large. I know no one will suffer. The worker will make up a new order for the customer who will wait an extra minute (or thirty seconds, they're fast) and I will walk away in ecstasy with my surprise bag of goodies. Someone though, no doubt a company man, will complain, "What if everybody did that?" The corporations would suffer huge losses that might put them out of business if it happened too often. I reply, "Everybody doesn't do that, only poor hungry souls like me."

20.

I have not even told you where I live. All this time and I've failed to mention it. I live in a gray city of distinctive architecture. Its distinction lies in its age. It's old. We seem to cherish old buildings, but not old people. We restore old buildings and prop them up and redo them and repaint them and try to maintain them in as near as possible to their original state as we can. We do that lovingly and with a budget. With old people we resent every Medicare cent invested as we try to inject life into their veins and attach them to machines that pump life into their lungs and insert needles and tubes (tubes into a tube, ha!) in their flesh, forcing life-giving substances to flow around. But we don't really value them. Once they get that wrinkled look and their hair fades it's all over. In our culture of youth we dismiss the aged, but not aged buildings. We lovingly seek to keep them with us as long as possible—those whose design we approve of, I mean. Others we blow all to hell and sweep away the dust, just like old people. But in this city where I live, old buildings are treasures. They have lasted. No matter that their facades are smeared with city soot, tinged black from smog and car exhaust. (We love old cars, too, but still, not old people.) Mountains rise outside of my city. Now, they are truly old. It seems like they've always been there. Most of us, I think, admire those old, old mountains, partly because they've been standing there so long. Old pieces of nature we truly love, but not old pieces of human nature. I think we truly despise old, old pieces of humanity. They are bent and they cough too much and their eyes seem hollow and they need help, too much help, our help. It would be better if old pieces of humanity simply passed away. But the mountains, they can stay. They can even show their age. We admire natural wonders that show their age, like those towering redwoods whose many rings tell you they are centuries old. Ha! I just thought of something. What if tree rings are the equivalent of people wrinkles? Century-old redwoods might not seem so majestic and beautiful if we thought of their rings as wrinkles. Let's not think that way. Buildings show their age. But if they don't crumble, if they remain standing—all with our help, of course, they need much attention—if their foundations do not give and they are repainted regularly (by us, of course!) we fawn over them and not only don't want to see them demolished, we won't let them go! No, we protest their loss and declare them National Landmarks. We hold onto them, even when their staircases will not support our weight and their use is reduced to a walking tour by people who cannot get enough of old buildings and will pay three dollars to be herded room to room, careful not cross into roped-off areas where the floor might give way. But the old structures in my city are mostly functional. The City Hall is the oldest building of them all. That is where I went to protest the traffic ticket I'd gotten. That car of mine had caused me so much trouble, I was glad to be rid of it. But the ticket I now carried around in my pocket, all crumpled and torn. I could have thrown it away, just tossed it in the trash, but I was not guilty. I had a time limit in which to pay the thing or appear in court and plead my case and I had chosen the latter. I was going to make a statement and clear my name, get the charge dismissed and not have to pay. After all, what good would it do me to pay a ticket on a car that no longer ran? That old City Hall building looked like Russia to me, old Russia before they killed Communism and replaced it with McDonalds. Russian leaders had, at one time, outlawed art of all kinds except portraits of themselves and works faithful to communism. The art of Russia had stalled somewhere in the early Twentieth Century. That was a most intriguing notion to me; an entire society could stall artistically and no new or modern art could be created. I suppose they had done something of the sort with their architecture as well. Their society always seemed caught in a time warp. But they

loved their old buildings, I guess, just as we do, and my city had
retained its old buildings in much the way that Russia had. Of
course, in my city they'd erected scores of modern buildings around
the older ones, so there was a difference. In fact, right across from
my ancient City Hall was a brand new mall—the proper symbol
of life here in the land of the free. But many said the new mall,
with all its modern conveniences and the latest building materials,
was ugly. Imagine that—old buildings were aesthetically pleasing
and new malls were gross. Did people consider the old buildings
ugly when they were first put up? If so, how did they become so
beautiful—strictly due to their age? Why can't people be evaluated
that way? Will malls be considered aesthetically pleasing in fifty or
a hundred years? Perhaps a Wal-Mart will be a sacred national
monument in the next century. I read somewhere (I do a lot of
reading; I think I read too much) about a hamburger stand that
was scheduled to be razed but was saved at the last moment and
declared a landmark instead. It was much more valuable vacant
than it ever was when serving fat-bloated patties with pickles. I,
myself, may have eaten there once.

     I should tell you that the room I rented was a dark hole with a
wood floor and high ceiling in one of this city's oldest homes. My
room's one window let in only thin rays of light, filtered through
constant clouds, and then through layers of smog. This old home
was a castle-like place, cavernous, with winding staircases and rooms
within rooms, and boarders came and went, some living their lives
unnoticed by me, down at the other end of the house. It was
halfway up the foothill of one of the ancient mountains I mentioned
and had an expansive yard full of sagging trees decades old and
crusted with moss. There was a pool in the estate but no one used
it and the water's surface had turned green. I do not know what
the pool bottom looked like, it could not be seen. A tennis court
bordered the pool, but with a rotted net and huge chunky holes in
the surface and no one used that either. My small quarters were
upstairs, as I said, and the downstairs had an airy dining room
with a long table and high-back chairs suited for a medieval king

and his court. But no one else ever ate at that table when I did. Often I would sit alone with twelve chairs and a view of the fireplace where no wood burned, next to a piano which no one played, and there I'd eat a sandwich of Spam, or a fat-patty on a bun, and drink tap water. I had to keep one ear open for my landlady who lived on the property. She didn't live in the castle full of rooms where boarders who did not know one another appeared and disappeared around corners and in stairwells. She had a modern, ranch-style house adjacent to the property, with central air and heat and mini-blinds. She was an old woman who lived in a brand new home. But she was a creepy, sneaky snake-like lady. She slithered and crept about and there was no telling when she might suddenly be blocking a doorway or waiting at the bottom of the stairs with a utility bill in one hand and a frown on her face. I had seen her several times watching and waiting for me. It had caused severe anxiety, as I've told you. I think I'd sweated permanent stains in my clothes. She wanted her money. I didn't have it. Twice I had to slip off to the other side of the great house to avoid her. One of those times I turned a corner in a deadly silent upstairs corridor and came face to face with a beautiful girl. I have been looking again for that girl but have not seen her. She may have moved away, or perhaps was someone else's guest that one time and I will never see her again. In either case she was a stunning thing, all milky white skin with ash blonde hair and wide blue eyes that fixed me with a startled stare before she ducked her head and hurried past without a word. I am unlucky with strangers, men or women, and have a hard time getting a word out. I must not appear friendly or approachable and I forget to smile. It is difficult to remember to smile when you are so filled with anxiety that your stomach muscles actually contort enough to pull the corners of your mouth down. That happens to me as I make my way to and from the hovel where I keep my few belongings. The fact that my car has died and sits rusting away on a city street works to my advantage now. My landlady can no longer peer through one slit of her mini-blinds, as I know she so often does, to see if my scarred and peeling monster

is in the long wide driveway. But I had fooled her before, parking
along the hillside and picking my way through bushes, then cutting
across the expansive lawn to get to the old castle house and upstairs
to my cell without being detected. She had caught me even then.
Parting thin leafy branches of a bush imagine the surprise, the
shock when her face thrust itself out at me, like some hideous
human lizard, and exclaimed, "Aha!" I had stumbled backward
and gotten twisted in the thorny morass. Tangled and unable to
move, picking tiny plant ends and dewy shoots off of me, she bore
down, her leathery face in mine and demanded the rent money
and the bills I owed and that I move my stuff from the room
immediately. I had crawled, actually crawled on my hands and
knees deep into the bush and out the other side and ran back
down the hillside to my car.

21.

I have noticed that we now throw pennies away. They lie in the street, at our feet, are left on tables, fall between cracks and are not fished out. They are everywhere and no one wants them. I went around picking up stray pennies one day (after I'd lost the gnat and was lonely) just to see how many I could find. I found sixty-seven in one day. I suppose if I were to ask every single stranger I met for one penny, just one penny, they would all give me one. Why not? Some might give me two. Some might be glad to hand me all their pennies. I'm not talking about begging or panhandling. I'm talking about conducting an experiment. I won't do it, because I don't talk to strangers. I don't talk to anyone, really. I even give away the pennies I find to old women and tramps. They take them and clutch them; but even some of them throw pennies down in disgust and give an angry look. Pennies! The nerve! Pennies are no good. They are the smallest amount of money. What can you buy with them? Not one thing. Nothing is a penny anymore, not even one piece of bubble gum. Pennies are good only for tax. So I am like a taxman, collecting pennies.

Small is no good. We like nothing small. Everything must be big, bigger, the biggest. Extra large. Super-size. (And you wonder why you're fat. I'm not fat. I'm reed thin from not eating.) That's why pennies are despised. They represent smallness. But I have discovered a joy in small things. The smallest things are sacred, though we kill small things without a second thought. We stamp out small bugs, and just about anything really that fits under our shoe. We don't blithely kill elephants. They're super-size. But ants are expendable, unnoticeable, really. Maybe that's it. If we don't notice it, it's worthless. You wouldn't kill a cat if it got in your way, though you may think less of it than you do of an ant. The damn cat is just too big to kill. It'd be messy as hell, too. Ants nearly disintegrate when squashed, or curl up when pinched and you can just flick them away. Yes, I admit, I've killed a few ants. No, I have no conscience about it. You see, in some ways I'm just like you. Some creatures I've actually pursued and crushed, like cockroaches. They inspire murder. Perhaps it's their appearance. We kill according to appearance in the animal and insect kingdoms. (Kingdom, what a word for expendable species we kill and eat and sometimes make pretty films about.) Puppies are cute and so are squirrels and otters are adorable. There are no good looking bugs. But we eat crazy looking life forms from undersea without a second thought. Some very pretty films are made of multi-tentacle creeping things with eyeballs on antennae, and after we marvel at their lifestyles we eat them. Cooked creatures smell better and no longer look like themselves, so they're tasty. Some very small things are tasty, like snails and fish eggs and even ants, with the right frosting. All this ruminating on dead things has made me hungry. Can you believe it? Thinking of insect corpses has inspired my appetite. I suppose I must forage for a meal, just like a creature in the animal kingdom. I must feed my tube or it will shrivel into an ever-smaller tube, and small things are no good (though I know better). To survive, I must eat. To eat, I must hunt. To hunt, I must move. To move, I usually use a car. But we know by now that I have no car anymore. So, to move now, I must walk. But why, why, am I walking around, walking miles, walking for food, walking, walking, with a traffic ticket in my pocket?

All right, I have stopped again, without eating again, still with a traffic ticket in my pocket. I take the frayed and sweaty thing out to remind myself of my violation. But it is runny with sweat and crumbly from my constant fingering of it, and I can no longer read what it says. A box has been marked but there the print is scraped and I don't know what I did. An amount has been checked off, but only the dollar sign is visible. Briefly, I wonder what a traffic ticket would taste like. I am weak from not eating. I am so weak I have forgotten what I am doing here in this life. You, I'm sure, are absolutely certain what you're here for, aren't you? That's what a good meal does. It instills strength and vitality and the ability to think clearly about major issues. So on your full stomach you have the answers, plus a good TV show, and dessert in the fridge (and a fridge, I must note) and you can lie back and contemplate your sacred and holy alliance with the universe, unless you have fallen asleep. That's actually what a good meal does to me, puts me to sleep. Every time I anticipate the luxury of a full stomach, so that then—THEN—I will have the energy to ponder the great mysteries all about us, I fall asleep. I think of how that rich soup or that fat sandwich or a steak or chops or drumsticks will allow me all night to figure out the whys and the whys and the whys. But then I stuff myself and burp and feel so content that I'm sure there is no mystery, that there's nothing at all to discern, that the solution to life's so-called puzzle is simple, simple, simplicity itself—it's a good dinner! But these moments of satiation come so infrequently that I am often over-boiled, running hot (like my car used to) feeding off fumes so that my head spins and my brain goes into overdrive. The wondrous swirl of creation all about me takes on a grandeur so infinitely complicated and at the same time amusing, so unfathomable and also so friendly, so multi-dimensional and yet so natural (as if I belonged here, as if there was no other place I could be) that it captures me, mesmerizes me, pulls me along like a salivating dog lusting after its bone. I've got to know more, I think, have to find out, must . . . arrive. But all that is sweetly resolved with a good burger and heaps of mashed potatoes. Thank God for butter and gravy. I could dunk my head in them and blow rich bubbles, force streams of it out my nose so that I taste and smell at once, so that I am glutted with pleasure. And if I could do it in front of a TV, why what could be better? Perhaps to have a woman stroking me, too. Oh, that must be the answer. To inhale butter and have gravy in my veins while mashed potatoes cascade over my skin and a woman's hands massage it all into me, so that it's mixed up into an orgasm. In the end I am melted soft gooey stuff that drains through the tube of existence without being a tube itself. That is what I want. That is the answer, to be butter, to be sauce, to be cream. But, God, oh God, what am I doing, what am I thinking. So long without food has caused this. I must eat.

22.

Small is no good I repeat, except for one category. Talk. That is where small rules. Small talk is all about us. It's comfortable, it's easy, it's non-committal, and it's fun. It's impossible for me. I have no ability for small talk. But small talk is a daily staple, like food. Anything beyond small talk arouses suspicion and sometimes anger. You are uncomfortable with talk that leads to thoughts and ideas and musings (about what it all means, sorry to inject that). Talk must be about the weather and what's to eat and the latest movie box office grosses. Small talk is so inconsequential and fleeting, so preposterous and meaningless, so trivial and forgetful that we love it, adore it. We lick our lips over it. It creates smiles and pleasant looks and great good feeling. We're sure it will not tax our minds or nudge us in the wrong mental direction. Small talk will not remind us that we are creatures of unknown origin spinning through a strange colorful existence that baffles us and defies explanation and is supposedly ruled over by a Supreme Being who may or may not resemble us and might spank us if we don't think of him at least once a week and on holidays. Small talk is our salvation. But I am incapable of small talk. For all my infatuation with things small, small talk simply will not come to me. Whenever I open my mouth, whether to strangers or people I know (though there are none of the latter left) I tend to pontificate on matters of the human condition. I see through the pretense of the everyday and recognize that Eternity is Right Now. How would you like to be confronted with something like that while you're doing your precious shopping or standing in line at the bank to withdraw money? I know, it reminds you of the boorish proselytizers who pass out religious pamphlets and orate loudly about

Jesus and Doom and Repentance, all while you're chatting to a passing acquaintance about whether or not the sun will come out. But that's not me. No, make no mistake. I am not trying to change anyone's mind. In fact, if I could change anyone's mind at all, it would be mine! Oh, if only I could talk passionately about the options on a new Ford Explorer or the won and loss record of that New York Yankee pitching phenom, but I can't. I open my mouth and only words about the nature of existence, consciousness, the meaning of it all, death and infinity come out. I realize you are concerned about that extra eighth of a percentage point hike in your mortgage rate, but I can't seem to focus on that myself without immediately being sucked into what it means to be human, to be alive, to be for real. It is an illness, an illness, I tell you. I want badly to discuss the new leg of subway being built downtown or whether loose or baggy is the current fashion in jeans, but my mind seems to go blank on these subjects. Or, worse yet, I find an analogy that makes a connection between some current and comfortable topic of discussion and my own outrageous ideas. Then I watch as the unsuspecting listener—usually someone on a park bench who has harmlessly happened to sit down near me and remark on the temperature—contorts his face, perplexed, perhaps frightened, at this madman (me) who can't just reply, "Yes, it is warm," but must instead remark upon the curiosity that air, itself, is always touching us, and that we, ourselves are always touching one thing or another—the ground, a bench, some food—so that all things are always connected, at every point, and there's no place where the connection is broken, and so that fact seems to indicate that the universe is one entity, entirely connected, touching itself everywhere at once, and that if this is so, every movement must (just like that over-used ripple in a pond theory) have influence on every other movement, and that even the smallest thing (even small talk, yes, even just a syllable, an "uh", or an "er") must reverberate throughout the body of the universe, and that this constant ebb and flow of movement never ceases, and that is why even the smallest thing is sacred, important, has meaning. Well, by then the listener has moved on to another bench and I am left with the birds. Yes, it's true; small talk is not my forte. I suppose I should drink. Bars and lounges and anywhere alcohol is served are much more receptive to my caliber of thinking. There, under sufficient influence of intoxicants, any kind of expansive stream of consciousness explorations are not only allowed, but considered appropriate, and worthy, too, at least until the booze wears off. It's actually not a bad thing. It's exciting really, to think that on just about every corner exists a counter with seating and the air there is open to discussion of the biggest ideas, the wildest notions, the meaning and origin of our lives, the reason we're here and why. Churches don't include such discussions; they just dictate terms and guidelines and give you prefabricated answers. I must spend more time in bars. Usually, though, you must lead in to your true topic with small talk, such as "hello," or "do you know the time," and that is the hard part for me. (Although that last one is a clever ploy which can segue right into "All time is Now, and every place is Here, etc. etc., which I believe, in case I haven't mentioned it yet.) But other topics tend to dominate bar talk, such as who had sex with who and who else, and how much the last politician embezzled and especially sports statistics. It's hard to get around these subjects, and since I am so uninformed about them I sputter out and get excluded from any conversation and end up my usual silent, solitary self. That is, when I go into bars at all, which is not often because I have no money to buy drinks. I am making a mental note at this moment to use the pennies I have collected to go into a bar and buy a drink and then at last I will be able to talk freely. Perhaps there will also be a free buffet.

23.

We are mortal creatures who return to the dust and ashes. We even name our children Dusty and Ashley (though no one, as far as I know, is named Corpsely or Remainsly.) Why, then, is everything so serious and important here? Can't I address you as the pile of dust you are surely soon to be? Why can't we laugh over the absurdity of it all? Is it not enough just to be, just to exist, just to recognize that we are alive, just to appreciate that we are experiencing.

I have heard tales of people who've had a brush with death, come so close they swore it was the end for them, and yet they lived. For a time afterwards they appreciated every tiny aspect of their lives—note the word "tiny" which is actually below small, but not quite minuscule. The little things became important to these people who'd had a brush with death. Why? Because they almost lost everything. They almost lost the big triumphs in life as well as the small pleasures. They instantly understood that any piece of life was precious, valuable, sacred. They attached a value to tiny-ness, great value. Even tiny-ness is above nothingness. But unless you have nearly died, tiny-ness is laughable and worthless.

I saw a man with scars on his neck and chest, tubes in his throat, gauze patches all over him, walking stiffly, herky-jerky, small steps, and smiling. I understood that smile. He was glad to be here, in any form. Something was better than nothing for him. Perhaps if each morning, everyone upon waking, was threatened with death—a lethal injection or a beheading or a gunshot to the chest—then spared, the rest of the day would be so beautiful, even if nothing at all happened. Even the smallest thing would appear wondrous. Each person might go so far as to embrace dust, or cherish a gnat. But this is too much; I've gone too far again. I don't want to have everyone threatened with death each day. I will not take action to create such a program. Don't worry, I will not write my congressman about it. I don't even vote, as I've told you. Do you think it would pass a vote, though? Would everyone agree to have their life threatened each day just so they could then appreciate what they had (and less)? I don't know. Perhaps it's a form of communism.

But what is nothingness and why are we so afraid of it? I, myself, am almost the definition of nothingness, if you look beyond my name. Luckily, my name proclaims grandiosity. It's like a storefront behind which there is only a stick propping it up. I'm very much like the Wizard of Oz. Except that I'm for real, at least in my own head. I have ideas and visions and I know how the universe works. I do not know how the world works. I'll admit that. Don't expect me to clue you in to hot tips on the stock market, or what will sell at the movies. Don't even ask me for directions. I am no help with the how-to's of life, how to keep your car running for instance, or how to choose and apply to the right kind of college. I know nothing about such matters. But the world and the universe are two different places. The latter I'm familiar with, actually on intimate terms with, and, as I've said, I think it likes me. I'm at its mercy, of course, we all are. But at least I admit it. I admit that it does me; I do not do it. I am humble and succumb to its will and do not possess hubris that might suggest I am the great thing happening here or I am in charge or I know how it all works and can connect the dots, or that I am in control. I do not assume any of these things for those notions are truly absurd. I am a pawn whether or not I think I am a king. That is the one thing I know. That puts me closer to the universe, so that we can wink at each other. Beyond that closeness is nothingness, the state we fear. But how can we fear a state of non-being? Who exists in nothingness to experience fear? In nothingness is no fear, no anything. There is no one. It is no place. If, when you reached nothingness, you knew you were nowhere, it wouldn't really be nothingness, do you see?

Anywhere where you can contemplate the possible reality of nothingness, the fear of it, the horror of it, is somewhere. In fact, the smallest place (actually, here we can use the word beyond tiny, the word "minuscule", perhaps even sub-atomic or molecular) is a place, is not nowhere, is a point, a dot (there it is!) from which to perceive the idea of nothingness. But even the idea of nothingness no longer exists once you reach nothingness. The ideas of things are not the things themselves. The idea of nothingness may scare you. Actual Nothingness contains no you to scare.

The closest material thing, I think, to nothingness, is a penny. Since people don't want their pennies, and they truly hate them, and will no longer even give them to babies to play with (because even babies deserve at least a nickel, and how long before we despise nickels?) I have hit upon the unique idea of taking pennies off people's hands. I am now an official penny collector. I pick them up in the street and I've found them in the grass. But I have gone a step further. I now ask people for their unwanted pennies. I do not panhandle or beg. That is not like me. I am not trying to make a living this way. I am conducting a sociological experiment. But I have stopped giving pennies to the homeless and destitute that block the sidewalk, lower property values and taint the view of beautiful old buildings. They are not receptive to the idea of pennies. They scoff and get angry, as I have said before. In fact, I, myself, have now been given pennies by the homeless. That should tell you something about the value of a penny, if even those with nothing hand them out. (There's an interesting concept: When you reach nothingness, you get a penny!) But I am going to change all that. I am going to use my pennies. I am going to make an example out of them, show the world what they can do. I am going to build a life, a new beginning out of pennies.

24.

I have had a serious setback. I tried to open a bank account with a penny and I was told to leave. I tried to invest my penny and a man in a suit chased me out of his financial services office. I came face to face with a rule that seems to be everywhere, a standard that must be met, a term called "minimums." Professional people do not reward simple ambition. My penny and I are not enough. I cannot even get started. They didn't seem to understand that I would grow my capital the same as everyone else. I would bring in another penny each day. In fact, I could guarantee it. They did not give me kind looks, even when I noticed a very shiny penny lying on the floor at their feet and claimed it, doubling my investment in one moment. That's when they called security. But I left willingly, even thankfully. I thanked them for a concept that I had not considered—at least not personally—minimums. I myself, was a minimum, the very least thing one could be and still be. I met the minimum requirement for life as a human being. It caused me to smile as I went walking out of that financial institution. For some reason, my smile was deemed derogatory, or snide, and security increased the pressure on my arm when I smiled, instead of wishing me a happy day. They didn't smile themselves, especially when I asked them, as I was escorted out, if they had pennies they hated and wanted to be rid of and would they like to give them to me. But the worst was yet to come. I decided to use my pennies to pay my landlady. Though she would not make needed repairs or improve conditions at my small upstairs room in the castle house, and even though I could not get into the room anymore and slept in bushes and with the night sky as my blanket, I would make a peace offering, I thought. This did not mean that my sociological experiment had failed. Yes, I was going to use the useless, stray pennies to pay off a personal obligation. But still my theory stuck. A penny was nothing, but nothing could be transformed into something. At least I thought so until I marched up to my landlady's door and rang the bell.

I am not sufficiently distracted by popular culture—media, movies and TV, number one hit tunes, ratings winners, the latest hip thing, trends, tabloids and Super Bowl champs. They have failed to divert my attention from this condition I'm in, that we're all in. Popular art forms and even forums on the issues of the day make no attempt to engage me in an examination of my condition (our condition). They just serve as distractions, mind candy, something to keep us occupied so we don't fall into the open abyss all about us. Basically, we do the hokey-pokey and turn ourselves around while all of creation—the mysteries of good and evil, the essence of life and the decay of death—ebb and flow in a constant miracle that we choose to ignore in favor of new earrings and the Play of the Day. The only minimum requirement is a one-day-a-week recognition that there's more to this cosmic mixture than fries or a convertible; in fact, it's all bizarrely out of our control and in the hands of angels. Then on Monday we go back to the snack of existence, the distractions, having had our main course and either digested it or threw it up. That is the regimen for believers, those who "got" religion. Many don't got religion and don't want it. But for most who got it, the minimum is fairly easy, with an occasional extra requirement for a holy day (read: holiday) and some nebulous avowal to work the concepts of church and God into their daily lives of TV and the mall. (Do malls have churches yet?) Others don't want religion and don't want any other concepts at all than TV and the mall and more money. But some don't want religion, yet still cherish the concepts and even contemplate them more than one day a week—sometimes in the middle of the week or even when the majority of the populace is focused on a particularly competitive golf event, and these people we label "out of it." (There are other, more extreme categories. I'm far, far down at that end. In fact, I'm beyond the end, where religion is not separate from existing, and so, holds no particular distinction, as obviously all things are religious, even TVs and malls, and no special requirement—not even a minimum of one-day-a-week devotion—is necessary in order to form a bond with the spiritual realm. In fact, you cannot break the bond with the spiritual realm.) But do you think this is a joy, to be constantly obsessed with the miracle of all of creation swirling all around, in and out and through me? Do you think it is easy to lead a day-to-day, conscious existence that is totally focused on the fact of being alive—that simple fact—as having more substance, more beauty, more relevance and more meaning than the grades I make on a biology quiz or whether or not I received any e-mail? Do you think it is comforting or reassuring to know where true importance resides? No, no, no, no, no! It makes me an outcast, a kook, a simpleton who is stupidly ignorant of the advantages of using STP in your gas tank or what that adored, best-selling pop diva named her love child. I can't tell you why I should buy Nike instead of Converse, or which is the correct fork for eating salad. I sometimes think I should be in hiding so as not to demonstrate my unawareness of all that others concentrate upon. But I can no longer get into my room and close the door behind me and huddle there with my thoughts and the knowledge that one place is as good as another and there really is no need to see Europe. My landlady has refused my pennies. Worse, she pelted me with them. That's right. She took them in her hand when I offered her payment for my room, and she screamed—a horrible cry that pierced me, grated on my bones. It made me understand in an instant that giving someone pennies is cause for murder. Then she whipped her arm forward and stung me in the face with my nonsensical offering.

25.

So now I am not back to Square One, I am at Square Minus One, for I fled without my pennies and have open cuts on my nose and beneath my eyes. But even so, I must mention (or have I said it already, excuse me if I repeat myself, I find that often no one is listening anyway and I can say the same thing over and over and over without reaction, or that even if people are listening, they don't seem to mind hearing the same thing over and over; they even like it—sameness is a safe concept) yes, I must tell you that I am all religions and none. That's right, I'm Catholic and Jewish and Buddhist and Protestant, Methodist and Episcopalian, Baptist and Mormon, Hindu and Muslim and Sufi (is that a religion?). And I'm all the rest, even ones I haven't heard of, even ones you've made up in your backyard, even cults and Pagan ceremonials and sacrificial ones—like Santeria and sex orgy religions whose names I can't recall—and any and every religion under the sun, or the moon and the stars. I am all religions, and I am none. I have no religion. I could walk down the street and into a temple or a mosque or a cathedral or one of those storefronts devoted to Jesus and bow down and pray, stand up and sing, eat their wafer, drink their blood, cross myself, clap, speak Latin, read from the Torah and the Koran and the Bible, praise angels and saints, shout hallelujah! mumble thanks, and drop pennies in a collection basket (at last, a place for pennies, in the surrogate hands of God, that great good accountant who will not refuse a cent). I know no boundaries of belief, no loyalty to one cloth or another, no reason to differentiate. I am, after all, a citizen of the universe. It's all the same to me. If I am feeling sufficiently devotional I need no particular, designated place to express myself. The world at large is my church. All of humanity is my religion. A lawn is an altar, a park bench my pew. The birds are the choir and the squirrels are attendants for the service. The sky with its sun and clouds and rays of light is a natural cathedral. My thoughts are the text, an intimate communion with spirit; no more intimate a union could be imagined. In fact, the service carries on even after I get up and walk on, you see, so that religion is everywhere. And I am blessed; I believe that.

To look at me you might not think so. My clothes are not quite rags but they have holes in them. My sneakers are worn to the point that my big toe can feel pebbles on the pavement, and sometimes I flinch and stagger, limping, when the sharp edge of one pierces nearly to the bone. But I was born with a naturally athletic physique (I used to be a player of sorts) and I walk upright, with wide shoulders (though one is sometimes sore from sleeping on it against pavement or packed dirt). I have slender arms and legs (a little too slender due to skipping meals) and a narrow face (streaked with hair now as all my razors are in my locked room). I'm handsome, I've been told (though I forget who told me) and my eyes have an intense quality (no surprise there), and I must add that I move gracefully, almost like a cat. I am watched over, as I might have mentioned, by an ever-present universe, and at the same time, I am watching it. We are one and the same, though at times I get the curious idea that I am separate.

At those times I'm liable to consider it greater, more powerful, more knowing and omniscient than me, and I'm likely even to worship it and allow that it is the originator and source of all the mysteries and fantastic occurrences that I cannot explain. But soon I come to my senses (my real senses, which begin with the sixth) and understand that I am not separate at all, and that I never could be, and that I am a partner, co-conspirator, and abettor, to all that happens to me. I then feel like a responsible citizen of the universe, paying my dues with each breath. I then am thankful for each day, each moment really, that passes in peace.

Some citizens of the universe never appreciate their peaceful

seconds, minutes, or hours. They need an especially strong jolt to
wake them up. For instance, survivors of a catastrophe—such as a
car accident or a twister—are always grateful to the Lord and state
to the news media that "God was watching over me," or "God was
with me" when their roof is sheared off but just misses their head
by inches, or their whole house blows away but they live, clinging
to a cellar door. When I hear that I muse, "Well yes, God was with
you (God is with everyone all the time and doesn't play favorites)
but you and God weren't having a good day. God also was with
me, and all the others who had a peaceful day and did not suffer a
near-death experience, but how many of us were so thankful for
that fact that we bowed down and kissed the earth?

In fact (my facts only, I cannot verify them and they are not
listed in any book) no one is separate from God. Eternity is here
and now. The curious truth is that you need to nearly get crushed
by a boulder or survive a plane crash to come to an understanding
of every day's value. And the general populace—those who have
no understanding of the all-encompassing value of each moment—
give great attention and significance to those who nearly die—yet
live, and to those who suffer sickness or disease that might kill
them but somehow come through it. We call these people survivors.
Yet those who never get ill or have no disease they beat or do not
fall from a moving train and crawl to a phone and push buttons
with a big toe to save them selves earn no attention at all. The best
they can boast is they were never sick a day in their life and never
went to a doctor, and we've all heard that tired claim. So what, is
the reply, good for you, you lucky bastard, but really, you have no
tale to tell, no book or magazine article to write. Who are you if
you've not gotten somehow beaten down by life, by cancer, by a
tumor or been in a severe accident and lived to tell your story?
You're nobody, you're normal; you're well. The healthy and happy
have no story. No, you must first get sick or afflicted, and recover,
to be a worthwhile story here. Why, it's almost worth swallowing
poison or inducing stages of bulimia just to get noticed—provided
you have the antidote for the poison close enough to gulp, or some

secret stash of Luscious Burgers in your drawer to give you the strength to write your book on how you nearly starved yourself to death.

I, myself am apparently crazy, and when I work myself back from the brink of insanity, to re-enter society as a nine-to five, tax-paying worker bee who volunteers time to disadvantaged children at Christmas, I will be a fascinating story. I will have gone from everything in my life falling apart, to pulling it all back together and rejoining the big show. We love that story. If I had never left the big show to wander stupidly like an idiot, mumbling and muttering about the great good universe as my friend and handing out despicable pennies to everyone, I would have no journey to make back, and thus, no potential book and movie deal. But you see, I am working on a career move with every wayward step I take. The further off the beaten path I tread, the more astounding my return to the everyday, workaday world. In fact, if I can reduce myself to the lowest level (the smallest thing—that again); if I can somehow descend to the depths of reality, no more present than a flea (a flea with a voice), and yet remain recognizably human (for someone has to witness my descent, has to peer close enough to identify me as this flea), I will have achieved the first half of this ambitious and clever plan. The second half will be my climb back to dignity—my ascent—my emergence from the shadows that claim so many, my conquering, persevering survival—triumph—to proclaim to the world that it can be done, that a man can lose all notions of himself, all reason, all semblance of being, everything, and still overcome it, still stand tall, a giant in the end. In the meantime, I have one penny left and have picked out a spot in the bushes to sleep tonight.

Now, does that sound like I have it all figured out? Truly, I squawk like I know it all. I have made ego-bloated statements full of hubris and conceit. I've become quite enamored with my own ideas and theories and even believe them myself. The truth is, that I may be completely wrong . . . about everything. Who am I to think that I know how to connect the dots? Maybe all my talk about dots and small things is ignorant babble (blissfully ignorant) and I'm actually in the dark about everything.

Perhaps this universe is stranger even than we can know, and numbskulls like me are barking up the wrong tree with confidence, with conviction. You'd probably do best to toss my tirade of philosophies, explanations, theories and guesses into a cesspool where it belongs. I myself would do best to shut my thoughts off, stop analyzing, cease applying my twisted logic to every moment and just find a job, some repetitive task like fastening plastic tops on prescription bottles as they spill out of a mold-maker in a factory full of Spanish speaking workers wearing hairnets. That way I could not think, just move my hands quickly, over and over, from top to bottle, and again and again, endlessly, forever, for there is no end to the pill takers in this world, always seeking relief or stimulation or something to move their bowels. In that way (that small way, sorry) I would serve the needs of fellow human beings, and perhaps need a pill myself to end the day and another to begin it, and eventually one or three during the workday, so that at least then my behavior would be understandable, popping pills and working, working and popping pills, snapping plastic tops on bottles, popping and snapping, pop pop pop, snap snap snap, and life would be no more than that, never an inkling that it should be more, as long as I was careful to simply eat on lunch break and not think, and as long as I could not remember my dreams.

The evening hours I could fill with more work (overtime, or a second job, perhaps sorting screws in a screw warehouse) and I could drink, as long as I was careful to go only to a bar where they passed the time playing darts and pool and watching football, and no one lingered in a dark corner spouting ideas and questioning the grand scheme of things. (What grand scheme? I'd say, and throw another dart). There's still time for me to switch over to that type of life. I've made a start, just by admitting that I don't know the answers, am not even sure of the question. I haven't led anyone astray yet, for no one listens to me. Certainly no one has quit their job or stopped throwing a dart just because of something I've said.

That's how little (little, ha) impact I've had on this world, that I could not, even with my most profound pontification, stop a dart from being tossed. My biggest idea is less (less) meaningful than a beer. Perhaps if I had something useful to contribute—like a wrinkle cream or a pill to lengthen the penis—my thoughts would be more valuable than beer, domestic beer at least. People would listen. But since I have no such valuable thoughts I would do best to occupy myself in some subservient way—washing windows or sweeping sidewalks—until I came up with a clever new way to lace shoes or a hair dye that did not wash out after three days.

Instead, I play detective with the evidence all about me and surmise that we, as humans, are actually spiritual and, as souls (one soul, actually), are immortal, and that we're all connected, all made of the same stuff—the stuff of the universe that also comprises rocks and clouds—and that there is nothing behind this scheme, no world beyond, no afterlife, but that this is the behind, this is the world beyond, this is the afterlife, and that there is nothing to attain, no where to go, no goal to reach, no reason to reach a goal, but no lack of meaning, no, nothing but meaning everywhere you turn, and ultimately, joy—that's it, joy, I've hit upon it in a split second, which is how joy arises—at being, here now, THE END. But we know that is not really the end . . . of this circle, for joy lasts only a second and is overtaken again by consternation, puzzlement, fits of sleeplessness, gnawing despair, a flood of abstract ideas about the world and its origins that can't be sorted out, and during this incremental befuddlement, in one irreversible moment comes catastrophe, everything goes wrong. Death and blackness and nothingness assail me. It's all over before I've discovered what it was to begin with, but somehow I go on, survive, subsisting on a particle of hope (the smallest thing) which somehow sustains me, grows into wonder, awe, a glimpse of the divine, a feeling that I'm on to something, a torrent of theories and explanations, all eclipsed in a bang with this joy, and then around again, and around, and around.

But enough of this, I have a ticket to deal with, though it is in two pieces now. It grew so crumbly and squashed in my pocket that it ripped in half. Still, I see that my court date is soon, in fact, it is today and I must hurry to City Hall, that grand old structure that pleases us with age.

Standing in the hallway of the court building reminded me that I used to be a successful executive. Can you believe it? I was not always this wandering idiot.

26.

It has happened. I have seen the inside of my head on the outside. Or rather, I heard it. I was walking, as usual, in public. (There's a curious notion: public, as opposed to private. In a moment I will show that they are both hallucinations.)

In one pocket I fingered my already worn and frayed traffic ticket, so soiled with sweat and grime from my constant anxious squeezing and gripping of it that it had now broken in two and lost a corner. In the other pocket I had left one penny from my disastrous attempt to pay my rent, one penny that had not come up when I'd fished the whole lot of them out for my landlady. That's how pennies accumulate, they get stuck in a pocket bottom or slide under the edge of the wood in a dresser drawer and so remain, cluttering all the lost corners of the universe with their nonsensical one-cent's worth. An empty drawer is better than a drawer opened that reveals a penny left in it. An empty pocket is better than one turned inside out to find Abe Lincoln (have you even looked, did you know it was him on that thing of distaste?) strangled by lint and dust. But of course, I had one in my pocket.

So there I was, on my way to the courthouse, finally, my mind in overdrive figuring how I would plead my case, but actually more concerned with how I'd appear when they saw what I'd done to their ticket. I worried that I might get another ticket for destroying the one they'd issued me. I planned to piece it back together for them if need be, just lay it right out on the judge's table there and show them how this crumb goes here and that crumb goes there and all in all it's my ticket, just like they gave it to me, nothing wrong. But I knew some crumbs of it might be missing. I, who knew the value of even the smallest thing, understood that a wise judge would also know that, and that the wise judge might point out to me how, even though I'd done a magnificent job of retaining all the loose crumbs of the ticket and putting them all in their proper places for the court, there was still a crumb absent and without it the ticket was not complete and the legal process would be forced to a halt due to this carelessness of mine. I even thought of possibly deceiving the court by adding a lint ball from my other pocket (if I could pry it off the penny) and passing it off as a part of the ticket. What might be the sentence for someone caught and convicted of such an offense—passing off common lint as an integral missing crumb to a disintegrated traffic ticket—I wondered. The thought of that scared me and I decided to take my chances with what I had, hoping for a benevolent judge. But I never got that far. Instead, my mind swirling with the story I'd tell and my hands clenching and unclenching the pulp that was now the ticket, I overheard a conversation on the sidewalk.

"Do you have the ticket?" asked a voice, not three feet from me.

There was a sense of urgency in it, and it repeated itself. I heard the word ticket clearly. Then, in the same instant, an answering voice mentioned the rent. I tried an old, cliché behavior—I tried to "collect my thoughts" because suddenly they seemed to be outside of my head. But the nearby voices went on about a ticket and the rent. I stared in the direction of the voices and moved that way, past a small crowd on the sidewalk, where I'd wandered into a particularly busy area. I was frenzied. Here it was, proof that my mind was not only inside my head, but outside as well. The exact things I was thinking about—things personal and known only to me, and of paramount importance to me, so much so that my life actually depended upon them both—were public discussion among strangers. The moment was frozen in my brain. There could be no other explanation. No one was really a stranger at all, and no thought was my own. Everyone was a part of my mind, and the only thing going on was my life, my existence, my thoughts, everywhere I looked! This is not a conceit, or some egomania. I did not want reality to be this way. I wanted to be like you, blissfully unaware of any larger picture, of any deeper state, of any hidden meanings, of any other dimension to existence. But, surprise! In a flash I knew the truth. We are all one, all one, like in a dream I had one time. A manic, screechy voice proclaimed that exact fact—we're all one, we're all one, it went on—until I awoke with a start, lying in some dark alley under a steady drizzle, and identified the tormenting, clairvoyant voice of my dream as a crying cat, its high-pitched yowl not the words I'd heard at all, just a cat cry, over and over, a cat cry.

What I hadn't counted on now was the action I would take. I had to congratulate myself, for I rushed toward the voices that spoke of the ticket and the rent. I went willingly right to them. I prepared to confront, not only them, but also the mask of the universe itself, and rip it off (Gleefully? Horrifically? Ironically? I don't know. Dangerously, perhaps). I was ready to face demons, to expose the underlying makeup of things, to once and for all define this thing that I am, and that you are, and that is everywhere at all times, so rich with ambiguity, so dense and unfathomable, so beautiful and rapturous and so inaccessible even though I and it are one. The ticket? The rent? You know what I have in my pockets, don't you? You know what I have in my mind? You are in my mind and in my pocket, aren't you? I was screaming by now, raving. All the attention of the street was on me. Two faces aghast at my approach and my accusations are now etched woefully in my memory (your memory, our memory).

As far as I know, and according to the accounts in the papers, I was dragged away laughing and shouting, giggling and crying, defiant and surrendering, struggling and relenting, mad because I was too sane. I see now, after calm reflection (and this is the only way to be, calm and reflecting) that it was all a trick I played on myself (that's the nature of this thing and this place, playing a bunch of games and tricks to keep yourself busy) and that those poor people I nearly assaulted weren't talking about me at all. They were standing at the entrance to a theater, searching their pockets for a lost ticket, to a very, very popular and recent hit musical that just so happened to be entitled "Rent." I know; it's ridiculous. Yes, I overreacted. Anyone listening to my raving explanation could only shake his head. The main result of all of this was that I missed my court date.

27.

While you relax at a round of golf or make plans to toast a new business partnership, I am seeking, seeking, seeking. I am surprised that the entire race—all the races—all human beings, are not down on their knees every moment praying. What the hell else is there, I ask, and I ask.

It is precisely because of what we all do here—our unnatural trivial pursuits devoted to making money and spending it—that I am compelled to bounce here and there, ricochet off one idea onto another, like the bouncing ball you follow to the old Disney song as the words play out across the screen. (It's a small world after all.) Only my words are the whys and the whys and the whys, and they do not rhyme and often don't make sense and have no real melody, only the steady humming sound of the universe at work, that eternal droning that accompanies reality. Stop, I want to say. Everyone (everybody, right) stop what you are doing, look up, reflect on what it is that you are, that we all are, that this phenomenon called life is. Then, go back, if you must, to what you were doing. We all have to make a living, of course. But perhaps some of you will not go back, just as I did not go back, cannot go back. That was my mistake, or the smartest thing I ever did—my big break, depending on how you look at it. I looked up.

That's right, I stopped what I was doing one day. Right in the middle of a perfectly normal (there was such a thing for me once) workday, I stopped and looked up. That doesn't mean it came about all of a sudden. I had been filled with thoughts and questions, quite near bursting with them, actually, for a very long time. Some of you might know what I'm talking about. I had controlled my doubts and my questions for all of my life up to that point, it seems. I knew they were there and I would come upon them every so often, and usually I'd treat them as mildly curious items of my imagination, playful ideas to give my working mind a breather once in a while, off-the-beaten path musings that filtered into my consciousness accidentally and had nothing to do with my real life, my real world, my career, the things I owned or would buy, the amount of money I had in the bank, my status at the company and reputation among co-workers, and my investments, pension and retirement account.

As I mentioned, as a successful worker bee I had never looked up, or looked up only once in a great while, and when I did it was just to smile and nod at the nice supply of sunlight allotted me and streaming down plentifully like it had been pre-ordered for my life, and to acknowledge my surrounding environment replete with just about everything else I needed to live, once again, like it had been ordered from a catalog and expressed to me, all for my convenience. How nice. What service. But I never thought to get the number of the service provider, just in case I might need this setting and all these supporting elements—like water and air and fruit trees—in case I decided to come back again, for another life. I did hear all about Him, as I've said, and the more I heard the more removed He became, sitting on a cloud somewhere, busy with another galaxy, hearing complaints on Sundays. I was comfortable with that. You must be, too. God, or whatever it is, is in its place, watching over the universe, and you are in yours, doing the work of the world, or playing a game of life. Never the twain shall meet, unless you have a near-death experience or, as in my case, you look up.

Now I know too much and cannot go back. I don't know how it is that I saw what I saw, but there's no mistake, God and I are one. You and I are one. You and I are God. The little (little) man, or woman, behind the curtain is me, or you. All the machinations of this great good and evil place are the results of you at the controls, or me. I know it now and it reveals itself at every turn, but try to point it out or corner it or define it and it slips away like mercury, a fleeting concept unable to be pinned down, an ever-changing, mutable, morph—able, constant disguise called reality. It is really best to leave it alone and not force conclusions on it and just giggle when it tickles you or moan when it puts you in a bind as firm as a wrestling hold. Best to be with it, though you cannot be anything other than with it. Even acting against it is a form of being with it. It is through and through, do you see? I should keep this all to myself, just listen for its whispers, and let it lead me where it pleases, but instead I've been unable to contain myself. I am overflowing with it.

I believe my filter has malfunctioned, though you probably don't know what I mean. I should, if I hope to lead a human life, be able to filter out the overwhelming knowledge of true reality—that we are all one and all connected and blah blah blah, what you've heard from me ad nauseam by now. I need to filter it out so that I can live and shop and go to theme parks. But even when I filter it out—for, as I said, I managed to for years, with only a few rays of gnawing discomfort getting through—I still see small hints, tiny clues, little telling details that all point to that larger reality as the reason I'm picking up on these leads. And if I follow their path I come to the realization that only the larger reality is true, only the grand scheme of things has meaning, that my shopping and that new eight-story roller coaster aren't sufficient reason for existence—and then where am I? Right back in its omnipresent palm, at its mercy, a connected dot, but like a jumping bean, full of anxiety and insecure about where I am and where I'm going. So you see, your filter must be very dense and not let a single clue through. One clue is all it takes and you are distracted (ha! distracted from the biggest distraction, this material life). Then a new feeling seeps into you, a feeling about yourself and reality that is quite provocative, a better game really than anything else, until you realize of course, that's it's not a game at all—it's the only reality, the final reality, the real reality. Better not to ever let it in. Better to keep your filter functioning expertly. Best never to know the nature of your filter, which is paradoxically the most integral part of this ultimate reality. It's like a spin-doctor, as they're called in the media. The filter is part of you telling yourself that the rest of you (the entire universe) is not really you at all. It's a good tool, this filter. I don't know how mine weakened and broke down, but like a frayed coffee filter, I am no longer getting just the juice of the bean, I am getting the grounds, and I'm afraid I'm getting too much stimulation. So this is a warning to any that are thinking of doing it. Prepare yourself for a much stronger dose of reality. You cannot look up and be unprepared. No, you will turn out like me if you do, and truly, no one wants that. But what it comes down to really, is that I'm talking to myself, even when I'm talking to you. The joke of it all, the cosmic joke is that I'm not even listening to myself.

Well, I think I've established my premise. I've explained it all in detail. I truly must get back to dealing with the concrete issues of my life. I'm no different from you, really. I have a mouth to feed and a home to keep (hopefully) and a few necessary possessions. You may be a businessman or an insurance salesman (there's a neat trick, taking money for catastrophes that will never happen, I should try that line of work) or an engineer or a secretary. I am an idealist, a philosopher of sorts. I ruminate and elaborate and often obfuscate the meaning of it all. You need me, because you are busy working at the tasks of the world and I am busy figuring the world out, including the parts we can't see. All I require is my daily bread, to sustain my tube, and I will go on chewing and thinking, thinking and chewing, digesting food and thoughts, excreting waste and ideas. My problem right now is that I am an unemployed philosopher. Have you ever heard of such a thing? No, they're called bums, or con men. No one is an unemployed philosopher. But that is my dilemma. I am Flex Ponderosa, idle dreamer (big dreamer) for no pay and no benefits. There is no value in what I do, at least to you. You laugh or scoff at what I do, or ignore me. I nod and almost smile at the station in life I've been relegated to. What could be more important than a man who constructs a big building (one that will get more beautiful as it ages)? What could be more essential than a man who knows how to give a fashionable haircut? What could be more vital and necessary than the boy who throws the newspaper or the man who repairs TVs? Not a philosopher, I know that. No, I rank far, far down the ladder of importance. I cannot leap high and stuff a ball through a net. That is value. Perhaps if I set my thoughts to music my philosophy would be more revered. Just three chords and I could get my message across. That's where most philosophy resides today, in hit songs. If I could just carry a tune and boil my premise down to four rhyming stanzas I could find work as a philosopher.

28.

I missed my court date. I arrived late and the grand old aesthetically pleasing yet crumbling courthouse building was dark and empty. I immediately scoped out a private corner, out of the wind and out of sight and curled up to sleep the night. I would have chosen soft grass under a tree but I am tired of bugs crawling on me at night. I panicked at first, when I'd awake to the feeling of a slight movement on my neck or in my hair, and jump out of sleep slapping madly at the thing, once or twice crushing the little crawler against me, or swiping some of its legs off. I could tolerate bugs, even befriend them, but could not stand them on me. Soon, though, I got less hostile, less jumpy, just shooed them away, as I figured, what harm could they do me, really? Other than the creepy sensation of having an insect upon you, what's the big deal? I have seen videos of people who let roaches scurry up and down their arms, men who allow swarms of bees to alight on them, all sorts of acts that would horrify most people. But other than the disgust, where's the real harm? And if you can get over the disgust, even enjoy the experience, then it proves that having bugs crawl on you is harmless.

I pondered briefly what some of these people, and others, do with their lives. There's an entire subculture of human beings devoted to studying animal and insect life. Some people follow bear families around the forests for years and years, for most of their lives. They film the bears and document bear life, watch how the bears eat and bathe and fight and nurture their young and then wait outside the cave where the bear sleeps for the whole winter. That is considered a worthy way to spend a life, watching a bear family. It's called valuable research. These people even become attached to the bears and don't want to leave them alone, ever. The same goes for birds and bird watchers, and for some fish, too. I often compare the life of a man who dons sixty pounds of underwater equipment and spends half his life on the sea bottom tracking the feeding habits of an obscure shellfish whose name I can't pronounce t my life. In that comparison I come out ahead.

Not that there isn't value to all lives, doing the most inane things, performing the most insignificant tasks. But at least I'm not swimming after a fish, I say to myself in these moments of reflection. I'm not bending over animal excrement to see which direction to walk, or following the sound of a woodpecker to see where ants live. It is sometimes amazing to me how people consider this a fine and worthy, even noble pursuit. It is like sightseeing, but taking notes.

Sightseeing is also very much approved of. Schedules are made, time is allotted, plane seats are reserved, guides are hired, and trips, treks, and excursions are made, all to see the sights. Not just any sights, not the ones in your own backyard, not the sight of your neighbor (for God's sake) or even the sight of your children's faces, but sights far, far away, usually very, very old, and often useless, except as sights. I am not putting these sights down, not at all. I am not under appreciative of sights and sightseeing at all. I am, in fact, totally in favor of it. It's just that I need no particular sight, with a particular history, in order to gaze in awe and wonder. I can look at anything, any street, any building, any person, and consider it sightseeing. Some are more exciting than others, true. But what kind of a thrill beats reality at every turn? A rushing waterfall or Grand Canyon is truly an immense sight. But the smallest sight (ah, there I go again) is just as mesmerizing. The same goes for animals, as bears are not an everyday sight and their lives are probably fun to explore. But what I'm saying is, I used to cringe at bugs crawling on me at night. Now I simply brush them off and then lie awake and watch them. They do all sorts of stupid and primitive and senseless things, about what you'd expect from a bug. But they are entertaining, just as entertaining as a bear really, and if I had a camera trained on them I would be considered a researcher instead of just a vagrant philosopher with no place to sleep.

Upon awaking in the morning I discovered the courthouse was closed for a holiday. It was a special observance though I wasn't clear which one. It had to do with someone's death, I think, as most holidays do. It was perhaps a day off in honor of one man, one former statesman or president who was shot, or in honor of hundreds of thousands, millions maybe, who perished in wars. In either case—the death of one or the death of millions—you only get one day off. Seems unfair, disproportionate. Remembering the deaths of millions should be good for two days off, at least.

But I have gotten holidays and their dates confused, so it may have been Halloween, if that is a holiday. Most holidays are retail events, I know by now. No one really gives much thought to who died so we could have a day off, except a few old soldiers who don their ill-fitting uniforms and give stiff salutes to a troop of young soldiers performing a boring ceremony under a blazing sun. The things we force ourselves to do. It makes for a sound bite on the news and then we're free to tally up the discounts we got on brand new merchandise (that will soon fall apart) all in the name of unknown dead people. The respect is staged, with markdowns and sales and twenty to thirty percent off, all accompanied by artist's renditions of the famous dead, and the flag, or some other upstanding symbol set above a prominent display of beer. Then we drink and toast and drink and praise and drink and fall asleep.

Because I had no money to shop (the markdowns did not fall to a penny) I decided to do my best to uphold the memory of the mortal immortals that served and/or fell so that we could enjoy red-hot price breaks. I made up my mind to occupy myself with the thought of these dearly departed, and the service they rendered all of us. I had only first to find out which holiday it was and then I would set my agenda for the entire day. This notion pleased me, as it relieved me momentarily of the existential burden I'd been carrying—seeing everything as a clue to an ultimately greater overall reality that consumed us—and instead, offered me the pleasure of sharing the same kind of typical daily experience everyone else uses to get through life one day at a time. But I could not find out what holiday it was. I asked several people on the street. Yes, I spoke up, buoyed by the camaraderie that spouts naturally from something as all consuming as a holiday. I knew this was information that everyone could appreciate and relate to. I knew my reference to today's holiday would make me welcome among strangers. I almost felt a social obligation to bring it up, to raise my voice, and let everyone know I was with them, one of them, a citizen, proud of our country's heritage and eager to bask in at least one small ray of history. But I met dumbfounded looks and stares and uninformed faces. Holiday? Is it a holiday, asked a few, giving me that look I'd seen on all the regular days, the look that said I was obviously a bit out of it. Of course it's a holiday, there's a sign right out in front of the courthouse that says so, I replied to their head shaking. But as I looked about me on the increasingly busy sidewalk it seemed that more and more people were going about their normal routines and not drinking at all.

I rushed to a store window where a banner proclaimed a sale and read the advertisement, which guaranteed a deal, and a rebate and a warranty and a free pen with a purchase, but nowhere did it say what holiday was the reason behind this generous giveaway. I was forced to get specific, ask pointed questions of passersby. Is it Christmas?! I asked to amazed and snickering looks. Is it Easter?! But I hadn't seen any evidence of either of these big retail events, no Santa or Baby Jesus, no Bunny or Resurrected Jesus rising from the dead (come to think of it, that image doesn't grace storefronts even though that's what Easter's all about). It was not Hanukkah or Passover I was told, but thanks for asking. Is it Mother's Day? No. Aha, Father's Day, then, that secondhand, understated day of new shirts and ties that somehow doesn't rank anywhere near Mother's Day. Why not, I thought. Sentiment, that's all. Holidays are sentiment and men brush sentiment off. But it was not even Father's Day. Quickly, and thanking each obliging person who stopped to answer me, I ran through all the holidays and found out it was not any of them. It was not Memorial or Labor Day, Not Independence or New Years Day. It was not Thanksgiving. Proud of my knowledge of holidays I inquired about immigrant ones, but it was not Cinco de Mayo, not Kwanzaa and not St. Patrick's Day. For God's sake—I used that expression—was it April Fool's Day? One person said yes, then laughed at me, playing an April Fool's Day joke on me when it wasn't even April Fools!

I stopped asking what holiday it was. What difference did it make to me anyway? Every day was a holiday to me now. I had every day off. I decided to make the best of it, though I felt left out, denied the simple, all-inclusive information that apparently was available if I just looked in the right place or spoke with the right person. I took some solace in knowing that there were many others who were as ignorant and uninformed as I was about something that seemed to concern us all and who went merrily about their way without even realizing the advantages they'd overlooked—the fact that they could have taken the day off and celebrated.

In a short time I felt less uncomfortable about not knowing what day it was, because so many others appeared unaffected by the same lack of knowledge. I even began to feel fine about it by about midday, as if I were one of them, the many who simply didn't know the truth and didn't care. By then I didn't care and I walked along sharing an indifferent expression with strangers who I could see shared my view. Inside I beamed with the knowledge that a holiday was passing and I didn't know which one and furthermore I wouldn't even mention it. I winked a few times to let the others know I was thinking the same as they were. But I encountered a few suspicious glances and that's when I really saw the light. These enlightened souls were not even thinking about not thinking about it. They truly didn't know, and did not even know that they didn't know. Oh, how I envied them, for now I felt guilty inside that I knew I didn't know which holiday it was. They hadn't even a clue that it was supposed to be a holiday. It was clear as a shining star on their faces and in their eyes. They were somewhere else all together. I wasn't one of them after all. In fact, I was completely alone again, I realized, for there was a group who knew what holiday it was and celebrated it, and a group who didn't even know it was a holiday, but only I knew it was a holiday and couldn't celebrate it because I didn't know what to do—give presents, dye eggs, drink green beer, or what? Yes, in the midst of all these suddenly kindred spirits I suddenly lost the connection and found myself an outcast again. It was a cruel holiday.

29.

Sometimes I talk to myself so loudly in my own head that if I pause for a moment and then go back to what I was thinking, I feel as if I was having a conversation with some real person. I even ask, whom was I just talking to? Was I speaking to someone? And all the while it was only me. The ironic thing is that, when I'm actually talking to some real person (an infrequent thing, but it has happened) I feel as if I'm talking to myself. I mean, I know I'm standing, facing another human being and they are either nodding and smiling, or edging away in uncontrolled anxiety at my appearance and my words, yet I'm thinking they are merely a device of sorts for me to communicate with myself. Wherever I go, wherever I turn, it's me, me, me.

My problem, as I see it (and it is a problem, make no mistake about that, I'm aware of my neuroses, just unable to control them) is that I cannot disconnect myself from everything else. As I've said, my filter has malfunctioned. I believe I am you as you are me as we are all together (to quote yet another popular song; pop philosophy is a big seller, but take away the music and all you have is poetry and that doesn't sell—we all know why—it comes too close to truth). But how do I live with this fact when the rest of me (you) seems to—on the surface—deny this theory, refute it? Underneath—in whispers and asides and knowing looks, in snickers and rolling eyes and sly grins, in tiny clues placed everywhere so I might discover them and spend my life trying to solve the great (supposed) mystery they point to—the real reality slides around behind me, sneaks up and taps me on the shoulder, sends me messages, plants undeniable evidence where I might find it, echoes from just out of my sight, maintains a presence all about me, but a disguise when I attempt to look it in the eyes.

I suppose a psychotherapist would say I'm paranoid. I've tapped into the left brain or something and I'm imagining that the whole universe is conscious, down to the last iota (there is no last iota, that's just an expression). I'm in what they call the one-down position, conjuring a daily monster that lurks within the day, within the real world, within the mind, my mind, which is everywhere. One step further into this dementia, the psychotherapist would tell me, and I'd descend into conspiracy theories. Everything is out to get me. But that's not exactly so. Instead, I believe everything is out to contact me. That's all. Just to let me know there's a greater phenomenon than shopping and championship wrestling. Just to let me in on the huge miracle that doesn't just surround me, but includes me. That is my response to the psychotherapist.

He (or she) is an intriguing action figure in this multi-layered package. The psychotherapist boasts years of training and valuable papers on the wall and has usually adopted a very respectable looking veneer including glasses and a clucking sound as he/she nods their head, smiling benevolently at poor sufferers such as I. They are here to officially deny paranoids like me, to soothe me into understanding that what I consider to be the nature of reality is nothing more than a hallucination brought on by job stress. I should thank them, and pay them well, and take their advice and try to believe it, for I would be better off that way. I should leave all the expertise to them and go eagerly back to work, calm and secure after their treatment (which could last a lifetime, I'm afraid) that the world is just how it appears. Everyone is separate; there are not intimate, cosmic connections everywhere, and my mind is not outside my head. I have seventy years, more or less, and I can go ahead and buy that burial plot—headstone included—and in the meantime, take the pleasure cruise to Puerto Vallarta. This brings up a topic I meant to mention. I believe I alluded to it but did not elaborate. Yes, you see, I did once have a prominent position in a very high-class business firm, but I failed to mention why I am no longer there.

PART 2

30.

I mentioned that I was a misfit, it's true, from very early on. I told you about the drug addicts. Understand that my world formed strangely, a perverse existence devoid of the norms most children learn. This is not so unusual. In one way or another it happens to many children, and I can firmly claim that I was not abused—though abandoned, yes, and neglected, okay, malnourished at times, and improperly clothed, certainly, though I grew used to going barefoot, even preferred it, shocked the parents of any friends I had when they saw me. So I learned a different set of values and for most of my life I survived just as I've illustrated in my rambling discourse here—simply, without shopping, cheap merchandise sufficing, ignorant of formalities, suspicious of rules, an outsider who often did not even know he was an outsider.

I was not unhappy with my lot. In fact, I considered myself smarter than the average bear. I was often self-satisfied with how I circumvented the usual way of doing things and instead did them my own way. I snickered occasionally at the obvious folly all around me—women desperate for a shiny brooch, men stuffed into constricting suits and tied up so that oxygen was nearly cut off. Absurd, I thought, all slaves to the clock and their own inflated desires. I was what they called a free spirit and I liked it that way. I extolled the uncluttered life and did not regret my gradual falling behind of all that is believed to be progress. That is not to say that I didn't have problems, for it was a struggle just to keep up, even at my low level, and as I said, I lived with a family of drug addicts, so lack was keen, and felt, and the end often seemed near. Yes, but that was what I'd been born into—living on the edge and uncertainty were a fact of every day. Do not force me to explain it, just imagine a life totally unlike your own.

The change came when tragedy prevailed and one of my dear, beloved drug-drenched and demented siblings died on the floor of the small house we shared. I will not go into the details, the toxin levels reported in the autopsy, the pall death cast, or the irony that a drug addict looks precisely in death as in life, seemingly out of it and immobile, just nodded off. I will also skip the painful aftertaste of death's effect, which caused not a waking up and new sobriety among the rest of the family of users, but the opposite, a plunge into the deep, as far in as the needle would go, chemical relief.

That day forced me away from them, not as an escape, but on a mission to save them all. Off I went into a world so unfamiliar and intoxicating it was as if I'd injected myself with an overdose of reality (another irony there, for I was as yet unaware of the real reality).

It was insane, what I went through, really. I left the small town I'd grown up in and left behind all the aspects of a simple life. My uncomplicated days riding a bicycle, reading at the library and delivering newspapers on a daily route to earn a few dimes suddenly spun out of control, into the screeching, rushing, twisted, clenched-teeth morass of big city life. An uncle had put in a good word for me at a large company and an appointment was set for me to interview. I rode a bus—just the beginning of what would seem like a year-long bus ride—for three days, or more I forget, enduring the rocking and shifting, exhaust fumes, constant boarding and disembarking, bags and baggage pulled and piled and hauled up and down, stopping and starting, nights and days, restaurant bathrooms. The romance of the road that they speak about, that I'd read about, was a lie. By the time I reached the big city on the edge of the continent I was a haggard mess, cramped and dizzy, like I'd been blindfolded, spun around and pushed downstairs with the directive, "Get a life!"

But I was so aggrieved and so committed I quickly adapted, learned new ways, stuck it out and there I landed, through some miracle or misunderstanding—either would be an acceptable explanation—at the company. I'd saved just enough to get a room, a bare room, that I did not notice was bare. Then I had my interview. By any measure I should have been denied the position. I was ragged, naive, unsophisticated. But two things worked in my favor—my uncle's referral (my uncle was a hard-working, self-made man and a hearty, good-natured personality) and my reading. Yes, it turned out that the officer of the company who screened me had read many of the same books I had. I don't remember how we started talking about books, but the job required research responsibilities. He overlooked my appearance and we discussed ideas. It was even pleasant. Unexpectedly, I enjoyed myself in this office. Even more unexpectedly, I was hired.

I tried to fit in from the very start, determined to open new doors, be all that I had never been before. Of course, I was stupidly out of fashion and still could not strip myself of ways I'd learned. I bought second-hand goods and marked-down clothes and tried to pass them off as office suitable. Instead I drew strange stares and snide comments, all of which didn't bother me. I laughed too, for I understood my own shortcomings in office procedures, office politics, and how appearances are important and must be kept up. Fortunes rise and fall upon the way one says hello or how a tie is tied (a major personal problem, for when I finally begrudged myself to wear one, I couldn't figure out how to loop the damn thing in and around and form one of those perfect, secure—and vitally essential for appearances—knots). I proudly picked a heavy, lumbering pair of black shoes from a thrift store rack for a dollar and bought a used black jacket which I wore every day. I failed to interpret that same half-confused, half-amused once-over I received from every company worker I met in my job duties as a scowl of derision, a disapproval rating waiting to be recorded, a point against me from the start.

I was pleased with my new self. Imagine, I'd been barefoot only a short time before. I was dressing up each day, and even felt new, as they say in How to Dress For Success seminars and tons of self-help and image makeover books—new clothes make a new you! It was working for me. Yet all about me I was the subject of jokes and whispers. Well, my clothes alone would have been sufficient reason to let me go, had I not proved to be more than capable, outstanding even at my job.

While I looked like a clown, my work was admired, even benefited the company nicely (read: financially). This led to more stares and remarks, for now I was singled out as surely a freak of some sort—all wrong but all right—see what I'm saying? My role was misfit. I stuck out like a sore thumb amidst the company men and women. As non-traditional as all my instincts were, I still attempted—at that time—to be a daily attendee of the human race. Yes, I showed up, even tried to join up.

There was pressure. There were sheep and a boss. I was expected to be like the sheep and I even tried to be a sheep. The boss was a fat woman, exceedingly fat, grossly fat. Her hips nearly did not fit between the armrests of a typical office chair. She wore loose, flowing outfits—tastefully tailored, expensive, very chic and contemporary— of immense proportions that could not disguise her shifting bulge, only present it as a flower-decorated waist, or two huge quivering thighs giving movement, flight even, to the butterfly design on yellow rayon. Co-workers could stop to admire the bird-ornamented material covering her arm as thick as a tree trunk. Her gobs of flesh covered gobs of malice, for at heart (was there one?) she was a mean spirit, jealous of anyone who showed an individual spark, playing lord over all the department sheep, but disgusted, too, at the cowards in her charge. All of her blackness, however, she covered with a sickening, sugary layer of sweetness, at once girlish and insincere, so that I was inclined to vomit in her presence.

Even so, I took the not-so-subtle clues of my co-workers and tried to emulate them, dress like them, act like them, be like them. It worked well for me and I almost succeeded in obliterating my former personality. I was raking in money, money that I hadn't even learned to spend yet, and heard myself saying yes to ideas I despised, yes to methods I judged (somewhere, in the back of my head) immoral, yes, yes, yes to corporate speak and corporate thought and corporate life. I could not have become more regimented had I joined the Army. But the boss lady didn't like me, because I was probably not a good enough imitation of a sheep, and I didn't like her, an acceptable feeling as long as you don't show it. But in between my bah, bah play acting I spoke some truth (and yes, the truth will set you free, as you'll see) and so she kept her witch-eye peeled for me, with an ear open for any stray whisper that would justify leading me to the slaughterhouse.

In the meantime, as I said, I accumulated money—an act judged as success, even if you never spend a penny. I was like a card player who hit multiple jackpots, kept circling the pot with his arms and raking it all in, but who never left the table. All I had were piles, riches waiting to be neatly stacked. Were they true riches, I wondered? I looked around for something worthy to spend my riches on. In the fast-paced merry-go-round of conformity I'd joined, and was now able to participate in (purchase, charge, buy!) I realized sameness permeates everything—our goods and appliances, our movies, popular books, TV and radio. It scared me and I was hesitant. I spoke to my fellow sheep (co-workers) and discovered not a single variation of the foods, toiletries, electronic gadgets and hourly schedules that governed them. I grew even more afraid. But I didn't let on, no. Instead, I discussed the latest with them, the latest this and the latest that, even though the latest anything was little different than the earlier versions. I pretended to be enthralled with mindless pabulum they claimed was movie entertainment, ludicrous overblown spectacles devoid of any comment on the human condition and requiring of the viewer no thought at all. I did not call their bluff. They were the majority and could not see the potential enrichment of free thought, could not, did not want to understand that alternatives existed. They opted instead for the acceleration of everything they already knew, forcing it to move faster in order to payoff bigger, and judging that as success.

I continued my effort to be more like them. I understood, I

told myself. We buy the same concepts of what it means to live and be human day after day in order to survive comfortably, in order not to stir up dust, to not make trouble, to keep uncertainty—and therefore, death—at bay.

But for me, it transpired in the reverse (what else is new). I actually reached a level of satisfaction where I had nothing left but to contemplate my own death. Yes, it's true. I needed so little, in the material sense, and was such a notoriously poor consumer, that I had all I wanted and cash left over and just looked around, wondering, what now? Death, the thought of it, the inevitable approaching, occurred to me immediately. Yes, I understood what the shopping was all about now. It kept death away, away from the shopper, away from the door, kept it out of sight, out of mind; do not introduce death into a bright sunny day or over a pleasant lunch. Provide a diversion, any distraction, more work even. And, wanting to be like the sheep, I too needed a distraction from death, life's party-pooper who simply will not leave the room. I found an adequate distraction right outside of the company door—my own bum.

He was tall and bearded, walked with a limp and ate anything I offered him, like some circus animal. He appeared in alleys and doorways, upon curbs and in parking lots, or might be right underfoot, asleep in the middle of the busy sidewalk at noon on a Tuesday. His clothes were soiled, torn, too large or too small. When he smiled, which he did often when I saw him, he revealed only a few blackened teeth. Most everyone but me ignored him. He had a shy, almost inaudible way of approaching strangers, pleading with his eyes but managing only a mumble, and most passed him without a look. But I was instantly, upon our first encounter, alert to this man and somewhat in awe of his condition.

Where I'd come from, my small town, there was no one wandering homeless and hungry. My own family was the bottom of the heap there, but they had a roof and curtains to close to hide their drug habits from the world. I looked at this man who walked with a limp and a grin. I don't know and never found out his

circumstances beyond the city blocks outside of my company
building. He appeared there as if from the dirt and stains on the
sidewalks, emerged like a breathing bag of trash that was in a pile
only a moment ago, now it had legs.

His solicitations were never direct, never accosting. Instead,
he greeted me like a pal, waved one large flat hand, and tilted his
head in a silly fashion under a backwards baseball cap. At first he
called me Sir and offered to clean my car windshield. He held a
pathetic spray bottle in one hand, plain water inside, no hint of
soap, no suds. I had a peculiar reaction. I saw myself. I mentally
retreated to a scene of myself standing among my co-workers, in
my laughable outfits. I experienced an extreme panic. But then I
recovered and allowed him to wash the windows on the used car
I'd bought after eight paychecks (Finally, off the bus!). When he
was done I gave him my jacket. That's right, I took off the
secondhand thing right there and handed it over to him, change
still in the pocket. He draped his grungy, dirt-caked frame with it
and jingled the coins, took them out and counted them, sixty-
three cents. He danced a few steps, squirt bottle in hand, toes
protruding from holes in his shoes.

The next time I saw him the jacket was gone, replaced by a
torn shirt. This time he called me Bro. No matter, I handed him
my socks and the leftover candy bar from an office celebration.
That became a steady habit, taking extra goodies from the birthday
groupings and holiday spreads that were a regular part of the office
life. Despite their obvious dislikes for each other, my co-workers
staged weekly get-togethers in the conference room, surrounded
by bowls of snacks and sodas, and fake talk ricocheted back and
forth until the treats were gone. The boss lady always showed up
surprised, her nose working overtime at the odor of pretzels and
cheese nachos, her fat hands digging for the most. But her eyes
never left the faces of her sheep, a curious habit, as she seemed to
defy us to acknowledge she was eating. But eat she did, with
insincere praise regarding our work, and future plans so ambitious
we staggered off under their weight. Always I filled my pockets

with chips and cookies and morsels for my bum, who became my
project. I wanted to nurse him to good health.

I continued to send steady sums to the drug addicts I called a
family, but still I had cash on my hands. I planned the day when
I would go shopping, and pictured the glossy items the sheep
bayed about daily. Yes, I'd pick out a few for myself one of these
days; I just could not set the date. Instead of a pleasure it seemed
a chore. I told you I was a misfit.

I contemplated asking the department secretary—an
experienced shopper with far more than she needed, who wore a
different outfit each day, seemingly disposing of a dress or suit
once it had been used, for I never saw it on her again. I thought
perhaps she could toss a few items in her cart for me. I even
approached her, jokingly, with that idea. I learned that she selected
items from catalogs and ordered them delivered to her and she
somewhat curtly suggested I do the same, and soon. I replied that
I would, but I didn't.

Instead, I thumbed through one of those men's catalogs and
tore out a picture of a well dressed, perfectly shaped, serious faced
man and showed it to my bum. He nodded his head enthusiastically
when I asked would he be interested in such a style of clothing. I
told him to fill out the order coupon and inside I grew excited at
the idea that I could salvage this man and renew him for a mere
two hundred dollars. Yes, a slew of makeover ideas occurred to me
on the spot, though I am not a viewer of talk shows and specials
that promote those kinds of things. He'd need a shower and a
shave and a new haircut, all of which seemed logical now that he'd
decided on Executive Elegance, the suit type in the photo.

But it turned out my bum did not know his own name and
could not complete the coupon. I suggested a name for him (this
was even before I'd selected a new name for myself!). He nodded
his head, but it was clear he had no intention of answering to it.
Still, I called him by his new name. Goldman I called him, because
I thought the imagery would make him feel valuable, Mr. Goldman,
to add a little respect. He didn't argue, only laughed, but do you

see the reasoning? I could have named him Poorman or Les Fruitful or something that seemed more appropriate but would actually be demeaning and detract from his self-image.

Finally now, I talked to my bum, my Mr. Goldman. We had, at first, only exchanged greetings and spent just enough time together for me to hand him something, then watch him hobble away with a smile. Now we spoke. His voice was heavy, a somewhat blubbery tongue. Perhaps from not speaking much he'd lost the use of it. He worked to pronounce his words and stared between them, reaching for thoughts.

"Every day is . . . a . . . miracle," he mumbled.

I recalled where I'd come from, how I longed for nothing much back then, how I missed nothing that I'd never had. Expectations, I still had none. A tough childhood, deprived of basic comforts and even food, leads to that—lowered expectations. But this also has its advantages. With lowered expectations, anything is greatly appreciated. If you don't expect to eat, a crumb of bread is wonderful, delicious. If you don't expect to be protected from the elements, then nice sunny weather is a blessing. If you don't expect friends and social activities, then kindness from a stranger is everything. If you don't expect to live, then not dying is a miracle to behold. I felt in my pocket and squeezed dollar bills, so precious now I could not do without them.

31.

Life at the firm was good in the time before I looked up. I was a hard worker, staying late, getting the job done. I even liked it. It enabled me to send money home, to the drug addicts, who I thought were rehabilitating them selves, because they told me so. But they weren't. They were spending every dime I sent on harder and stronger and more potent chemicals. If you know drug addicts at all you know better than to believe anything they say. I knew them well, too well. I was (still am) related to them. That clouded my judgment. I believed what the drug addicts said, their promises, and lies. I lived a fairy-tale existence believing they were getting better.

In the same (fairy tale) fashion, I watched her at the job. Her name was Erin and I believed she noticed me, too. I had a simple thought in mind. I wanted to tell someone that I loved them. I don't know where this thought came from. But one day it seemed to be an overwhelmingly important thing to do. I was actually aghast that I might go through an entire life without expressing that thought—in its purest, most meaningful form—to someone. So that is all I wanted to do, to tell someone (other than a gnat) that I loved them. It turned out to be the most troublesome notion that ever entered my mind. It turned out to be my undoing.

You cannot simply decide one day that you love someone. Though I'll admit, love can strike one unaware, at a moment's notice. The problem was, I wasn't struck like that. I wasn't dizzy with infatuation, lightheaded, elated with emotion. I was, instead, determined. Can you understand that? For it is an absurdity contradictory to the idea of love. I was determined to make a connection—to express what I had suddenly come to understand was the true grounds of the universe. She was, in a sense, more the object of my determination than the object of my affection. But at the time I didn't know that. Do you still follow me? I didn't know that I'd merely selected her for what I now perceived was the highest calling of a human being. I convinced myself of more than that. I convinced myself that she was the one for me. That is the saddest part. For, if there is nothing nobler, more meaningful than true love and the act of imparting that to another, then there is nothing sadder, nothing more empty than attempting—no, no, not just attempting, but going through all the motions, playing the role completely, to the hilt, the whole nine yards as they say—nothing sadder than pretending to all this when, in fact, the love does not exist.

That's not to say there weren't good feelings, and fun, and the best of intentions. But you can't manufacture love. And when it isn't present there's a giant obvious hole. She was a good girl, a special girl, a co-worker with a dazzling smile and very pretty lips who shared pleasant exchanges and courteous interactions with me, all before I looked up and realized love was the vital nature of all existence and demanded my whole being address it.

I think, perhaps, I should have quickly looked back down, buried my head in my work and never given another thought to this revelation that so overwhelmed me in a fraction of a second. Where had it even come from? I've said, and it's true, that notions had seeped into my head for years and years, notions about what it all meant and what I was here for. But I'd only entertained those notions as curiosities, time fillers to accompany lunch, idle grazing on the grass of life that grew all about me. Figuring it all out was not my job. I suppose I expected to read in the papers or hear about it on the news when, indeed, someone whose job it was—a priest or a scientist—had finally reached a conclusion and could let the rest of us in on what he knew. I mean, sure, those types offered up answers and solutions of all kinds, all the time. But no one ever really came out and said, "Aha! Here it is, the one and only real truth. The one real thing beyond which nothing else really matters. And here's what you do, how you do it, exactly, so that there's no more question, no mystery, no loose ends!" Weren't we all awaiting just such a moment? And then, in the midst of another regular day, at no special hour and under no extraordinary circumstances, I was visited by the startling concept that I was the one. Not a priest or a scientist or a three-year-old Indian boy deemed the incarnation of Buddha, but me. Not a motivational speaker, or an old grandfather who'd never smoked or taken a drink, or a philosophy professor on staff at Harvard, but me. I was the one who possessed the singular knowledge, the secret—the key to the soul. (Of course, I didn't think at the time that we all have this key, I thought only I had it.)

Unfortunately, I was not sophisticated enough to know what to do with my newfound knowledge, my enlightenment, let's call it. I wasn't savvy, wasn't capitalist enough to immediately establish myself as a New Age guru to bored, complacent, dissatisfied or underachieving types who would pay me well to let them in on my secret. No, I wasn't smart about it at all. I could have begun my own enlightenment correspondence course and made a small fortune with the right placement of classified ads in the back sections of tabloids and supermarket magazines. I could have gone further even, created my own infomercial, accompanied by an audiotape in two sets, sixteen parts, that would slowly and hypnotically unfold the simple truth that I had stumbled upon— or rather, that I had ferreted out of the universe itself through intense investigation and contemplation. No, I was not a marketing genius and did not perceive the potential that had fallen into my lap. I did not seize the opportunity, did not seize the day. I did not use the concept to make money. Instead, I marveled at how a minor shift in consciousness had changed everything for me, everything, and I treated it very seriously.

I took it personally, you see, and allowed that it was important, and that I was important, and that the whole grand scheme of things, of life and existence, was important. I could have made a million by now if I hadn't deemed it—this new knowledge like ripe fruit—so essential, so vital. If I had treated it like a product to be exploited I would be a rich man. Others would flock to me and pay dearly for each little clue, each crumb I would hand out. And though the truth itself seems so simple, the way to it is endless, eternal really, is comprised of every little thing along the way—and I mean that, I mean every single little, tiny, minuscule particle of reality plays a part. The whole of it, the whole true rich oneness, can be traced down to the trillionth of an iota, without which it all would not be complete. But it would take the full set of audiotapes to get to that fact, and probably another, new round of tapes to explain that and how that trillionth of an iota affects you, and of course, how all the dots connect.

But instead of determining a business plan to reach the multitudes—and it would have had humanitarian, even altruistic merit, this disseminating of truth and knowledge to the hungry ignoramuses of the world—no instead, I focused in on the startling reality and how it had irreversibly changed me, so quickly, in a moment, and how I needed to serve this new truth.

That's it. That's the problem in a nutshell (another small container of truth). I had perceived myself as the servant of my revelatory state, instead of as the master. Had I seen myself as master, I would have a book on the shelves and a lecture tour in full swing now. I would be generously telling you what my research had uncovered. From me you would learn how to live anew, how to see the world anew, how to be real. I would point out your oh-so-common human errors, your faulty thinking, and your misconception of the true nature of existence. You would listen carefully and ask humble questions at my seminars. Magnanimously, I would give you answers so simple they'd seem mysterious, complicated, and full of hidden meaning. We would all go away happy, me rich and you still searching, searching, for what I had, but certain now that you could have it too, by the end of the next audiotape. You would tell your friends, and they would tell their friends and soon I wouldn't even have to advertise. Soon I would be a brand name. Flex Ponderosa, Master. My name would become associated with all things cosmic. My name upon a product would transform it into a conveyor of new consciousness. There would be Flex Ponderosa cereal and Flex Ponderosa bathing suits, and perhaps a Flex-Mex burrito and Ponderosa software for computers. That power underscored the new me—the me who had looked up. A pity, though, I had no real sales background.

32.

What is beautiful? What is true beauty? We have transformed the concept of beauty. We now think of towering, glimmering, fantastic skyscrapers as beautiful. Yes, we stare at mixtures of cement and offer praise. Or we run our hands over the streamlined contours of an automobile, tingling with pleasure at the sculpted bodywork, admiring its aesthetic form. Cars are beautiful, too. (Even sexy, they're advertised as sexy. How did that come about? How did objects of metal, glass and rubber, filled with a toxic chemical like gasoline, become sexy?)

We so revere our concrete and our asphalt that we are forbidden to throw paper on it. That is a crime. Littering on beauty. Our cities full of blaring, blinking, billboard-sized signs, all lighted up and bombarding us with messages are off limits to spray-painted slogans. That, too, is a crime. You cannot graffiti graffiti, if you see what I mean. The correct kind of graffiti was there first, so the vulgar graffiti out of a spray can is not allowed to taint the original graffiti.

What about blue water and green grass? That is beauty to me. What happened to them? The blue water has been blackened and polluted. The green grass is now pavement. They paved paradise and put up a parking lot, to quote another pop song (the last bastion of modern-day philosophy, the last appeal to common sense and decency). But I did not always realize the pure beauty of blue water and green grass. Oh yeah, I gazed in awe at the ocean like you, and I rolled down little knolls at the local park like you, or spread a picnic blanket over comfy soft cushiony blades, or settled down with my drink to the serene vista of a mountain lake's surface. But these were vacations, weekends, day trips, and time off. I expected to find some brief interlude from the concrete, and nature served its purpose for a working professional such as I. That's what I was, a working professional who had been sucked in to the illusion of majesty offered by taller buildings, especially with great glass facades. I trampled grass and fouled blue water (the only blue water I found, the artificial toilet bowl kind). What were they to me? They were there to be used, God's supplies (remember, what service!). Until, I looked at Erin and saw beauty.

She was not beautiful in the magazine, TV and movie sense. She had not done anything artificial to herself to enhance her looks, though she used lipstick quite creatively. To a pageant judge she would have finished out of the running. But I had not looked at her the way a pageant judge would. I'd seen her as a beautiful human being. I know how ridiculous, how high-minded that sounds. I'm not pretending she had no genitalia. I'm not likening her to a saint or some asexual goddess. In fact, it was her true humanity, her base, physical functioning self that constituted much of her beauty. You see, it was her essence, the make-up of her, and the fact that she was a mortal, temporary thing that held such fascination for me. Well, what then of everyone else? Aren't we all mortal temporary things slowly disintegrating right in front of each other? The answer is yes, and the next question is why then, her, why not just anyone, and the answer is—she was just anyone, do you see? I had looked up and seen the all-encompassing oneness and realized I needed to love it and tell it I loved it. The next thing I saw was her, my fellow worker and she became the worldly focus of my sudden and brand new purpose and nothing else mattered anymore. She was new green grass and fresh blue water come alive, animated, walking and talking and smiling.

I'd made a mistake, because as I've said you cannot decide to love someone. I had not decided to love all of humanity, all of the universe, all of it. Rather, all of it had overcome me. Erin was just the representation of my longing, of my incomplete soul, of my need to physically express what had happened to me on the inside. But I am sick of my own babble. I sound like a fool twisting in a romantic wind. I must face facts, hard facts, reality, as it exists for you and others, the real world as we know it. I started out with pure universal love in mind, with a vision of a wonderful magic she and I could share and I ended up pulling an innocent soul down into a black abyss. That was not how things were supposed to go. My sixteen-part audiotape would make no mention of a black abyss. But in fact, there is a flip side, a darker side to all of this awesome enlightenment I've been touting. I'm not supposed to mention it. It doesn't sell, except when cleverly packaged as a spook show of sorts, one that can be turned off when it gets too intense. But the real dark side cannot be turned off. The real dark side is the dousing of the light, quashed hope.

Remember hope, the incremental phenomenon I liken to despair, also an incremental phenomenon? Well, hope dissolves incrementally as despair grows. Little by little, if you'll excuse the expression, one replaces the other. You understand, it's in the shadings, very subtle, so that you can't quite see it happening. I did feel it though. But I didn't know what it was at the time. I had awakened into the world of light and wanted to spread it, to touch another with what had touched me. At first that's what happened, or so I thought. But at some turn it dimmed, and from there began to fade, until the light was far away, farther than it had been even before I knew of it, farther away now because I did know of it, knew where to look for it and thus knew its glow had diminished. I could never have plunged into the abyss had I not seen the light to begin with. It begins to sound trite—It is better to have loved and lost than to never blah blah blah . . .

But you see, there was a turning point when I realized I had fooled myself, had gone off the deep end. I realized that I did not love her in the sense she expected from me, from a man. She had been so good, curiously receptive to me at first, then trusting, and finally, in only a relatively short time, wholly committed and, I think, in love with me. And why not? What did I do to discourage it? Nothing. I feasted upon her, reveled in her attention, made a mad glutton of myself, slurping her emotion, savoring the fact of

her in my life. The high-minded, pure love I envisioned and felt I
needed to express quickly compromised itself in physical and
sensual pleasures.

33.

The office where I worked was in a tall building, very modern, and admired by passersby for its height. It sat along a corridor of similar grand structures all in a row, standing triumphant like royal, outsized chess pieces. Erin and I could not wait for the workday to end, so that we could make our sweet escape. Then we hurried along the sidewalk, exhilarated by air, by touching fingertips. One by one we found the getaways and hideaways, cozy corner booths in downstairs back room restaurants, neatly tucked within ground floors of these twenty and thirty story creatures.

There we dined and drank, lingered over plates full of meat and gravy, heads spinning with alcohol and lust. And why not? I made a good salary and at the time my car ran well, the paint still intact, the radio producing full-bodied music from both speakers. We relished time together and embellished time with the satisfactions of the human body, the elixirs of the human mind.

I didn't take her to church, didn't plan a spiritual journey to see the Dalai Lama; didn't suggest we run away together with the Hare Krishna's. I had no goal in mind, no conversion of her way of thinking to mine. In fact, I may have lost sight of my own way of thinking soon after entering into the liaison with her. I was having a grand time, oblivious to it all, to the cares of the mortal world, to the larger picture. I even forgot, for a time, the incredulous moment that had ushered me to her, to this fine interval of laughter and kissing. Maybe it was all my mistake, and nothing more serious had occurred to me than I'd been shot with Cupid's arrow. But slowly (incrementally) I began to recognize my error.

Oh, in between that were raucous good times and sex so dirty and base I can still smell it. We went to her little place above a courtyard in a nearby seaside village. With the windows cracked, inviting the ocean breeze and the last glint of a descending ruby sun, the neighbors will never forget our loud wrestling and hours of moans. I will never forget them. I did it all with my eyes open, wanting to see, see, see it all. She was my picture, a pixie with full lips and breasts thrust forward to meet me. Her eyes smiled mischief. Her arching body moved to meet mine. Her whimpers struck some resonant chord in me, somewhere deep down, something that wanted to cry in pleasure, cry in satisfaction, cry for joy. I swear I believe I existed in an inside world made of her breathy prompts and completed by my guttural responses. All became a sensuous echo and made me forget that there was a world just outside the window.

But inside something nagged me, would not go away, like the coo of a particular bird I have heard in the early mornings at many different places on Earth. I still do not know what bird it is, but it must be a fairly common one. Its soft, droning coo seems almost to follow me place to place, or else that damn kind of bird is in every other tree. I have never seen the actual bird. But always, always I hear its haunting sound, never altered, the same cool, calm tone, a few notes of it at a time and then silence, then, when you think perhaps its gone, another few throaty coos, to let you know it has not gone away. That bird is like a beacon, a lookout for the invisible world, a reminder, constantly, provocatively seducing my thoughts back to the greater reality, the bigger picture, the fact that we are all one, connected, spirit. So it was with the thought in the back of my head the whole time she and I were together, even in the midst of ludicrous, offensive (to the neighbors) sex, there floated the notion that I had made an error.

34.

Sometimes I consider the lucky dead and all they no longer have to go through and I envy them. The lucky dead are through answering knocks and rings, through reporting here or there on time, done with aches and ailments, cares and concerns. The lucky dead have no car stalled on the side of the road, no nagging landlady, no tattered traffic ticket to pay. They are free of the world, of the body, of the mind. The lucky dead no longer care and can't be concerned. If only we could live like that, like a dead person. But what am I saying? Until I changed my name I was like a dead person.

My name change is a sign of my own resurrection. I have come back to the living (maybe it is Easter, after all) and, incrementally, I know I can move forward into the fullness of the light once again. I am on a path, a mission to do just that. I know I get sidetracked and go off on tangents of regret and guilt. I know I made a mistake with Erin. I misjudged her, misjudged myself, and misjudged reality. It turned into a sordid mess, really. It was no secret, believe me, we could not keep it a secret; I did not even want to keep it a secret. In fact, I gave myself over to her, to it—the all-consuming new oneness I'd suddenly experienced.

My attitude changed and people noticed. Oh yes, I was bubblier. I was happy. I was joyous. Joy arrived quickly, almost at once, and why not. I had relieved myself of the drudgery of work and replaced it with the magic of love, all in the time it takes to double-click on a brand new program. Yes, I was abruptly alive and empowered with a new vision and she was part of it. Joy was everywhere, or so I thought.

What really happened was that my work suffered, my

concentration was broken, my performance was lacking and I was acting like a teenager on spring break. But I saw nothing wrong with all of this. I was pleased to have everyone in on my newfound joy. I thought I radiated a personal miracle each day as I continued my duties at the office. I was certain I was bringing a whopping positive force to bear all about me. I briefly considered myself deserving of a raise just because my effortless goodwill was rubbing off on the other employees. I lived in a bubble of joy that was expanding all the time. I hardly noticed the two-hour lunches when Erin and I would escape to a local park and lie together in front of a spurting fountain. I didn't time the snack breaks and coffee breaks where we lingered together for too long over a muffin. I couldn't read the true expressions on the faces of fellow employees who seemed to greet me the same and work alongside me just as before.

But if I would have looked more keenly I might have noticed their raised eyebrows and sniffs and whispers. I might have perceived silences that began upon my entry into a co-worker's cubicle, or the sudden hang-up of a phone as I turned a corner and arrived at a secretary's desk. I worked on a busy floor, partitioned every few feet by those insufferable moveable walls, and stares found their way between cracks; heads were cocked just so, ears positioned, daggers poised. Fool that I was, I interpreted every nuance as receptive, welcoming. Everything and everyone was part of my new good feeling. That's what I wanted—whether consciously or not—to share my glow.

Yes, joy arrives suddenly, with the onset of a big event, as I had experienced the moment I looked up. From that moment, joy surrounded me, enveloped me, and infused me. But in this world of opposites, catastrophe was not far behind. It, too, comes quickly, without notice, with the onset of another big event. But I am getting ahead of myself here, too far ahead. Nothing happens without a reason and there was good reason for the catastrophe that sank me.

35.

We close the door on excitement, discovery and the value of thinking new thought, as a means of protection, self-preservation. I have learned that the only valuable existence is one that is safe, secure, paid for, replete with comfort and left unchallenged. I was learning the corporate way and it was sticking to me! Truly, the most useless and distasteful event of a day is a new thought!

But regardless, in spite of it all, no matter how I tried, anyway, there's no excusing it, no denying it—I admit, I surrender—I could not help but be true (true, hah!) to my misfit self—I had a new thought. I tried to be on guard, watch out, suppress them, but one seeped in, and it was a doozy! Like a fool I looked up.

Yes, well, we've been through that and my sudden awareness of all that was truly important, essential. I've told you about her and our lovely frolicking, and about my glee so palpable I became immune (in my own mind) to any rules and regulations or standards there at the company (of which there were many, and strictly enforced daily). So, you get the picture and the result of all this should not surprise you.

The boss lady was jealous. It was in her eyes, in her hard stare, in her phony smiles. She saw that things came perhaps too easily for an unsophisticated poor dresser like me. I did not know the ins and outs of the business world. I had little experience in those marble hallways, amidst those sparkling personalities. The men in their tailored suits and shiny spectacles, and the women in their competing suits carrying briefcases and bulging portfolios blended well with the beautiful building interiors. They appeared comfortable, even part of the interior designs that streamlined each suite, achieved a mannered perfection—order—in each office and along every hallway. Their own behavior was in line with the environment that had been created around them. No word or look was out of place. Nothing vulgar or distasteful was permitted. All images were surface fresh and surface clean, betraying no hint of the construction beneath, or the eventual dust from which it had begun and to which it must return. These business-people were minor architectural and programming achievements themselves, having filtered out the more human aspects, or rather, kept them hidden, and succeeded at the art of presentation. They'd crafted social selves, workplace selves, professional selves who followed a noble code of conduct and dressed the part. It was all an admirable facade, a daily game, cosmetic camaraderie for the work hours.

But it couldn't be sustained, and indeed, the opposite element was built in to the model—that is, they were obviously all full of crap and eager to prove it about everyone else but themselves. So, of course there was gossip and hushed talk, backstabbing and innuendo, lies and complaints and attacks on each other, most if not all done quietly, out of sight, even in the guise of duty. The boss lady was a big player, of course, the target of ploys herself, but a regular missile launcher and I became one of her targets.

She began to pile work on me, forcing me to stay late, even to cancel dates with Erin. She did it with a particular viciousness, masked by her girlish plea, "Could you p-wease help out with this extra project tonight . . .?" I almost puked just watching the words form within her rubbery lips. It occurred to me that the woman was so fat her lips were overweight. Momentarily, I wondered how much effort it took to maintain such proportion. She must make daily, even hourly decisions just to keep her bulk so immense. It wasn't a condition that anyone could arrive at naturally, without some forethought. Her fat was premeditated. I tried to calculate how much of her consciousness was devoted to thoughts of food, how many 'bytes' per second coursed through her computer-brain. It seemed, with her tremendous fleshy folds, inconceivable that her mouth had time for words. But I knew my temporary focus on her weight was only a reaction to her attitude toward me. I didn't care about her weight. She could eat in her sleep if she wanted. The measurement of a person had nothing to do with a scale. But once she targeted me I resented her. We continued to treat each other respectfully, though.

Erin, for her part, was a joy. She stayed late with me, shared a snack or a dinner ordered in, and talked a storm about the bitch boss. The sheep had been gathering and voicing their own growing displeasure, she said. They were all unhappy with their treatment. Some were writing secret complaints, others threatening to go 'upstairs' to the head honchos, everyone in agreement that something had to be done about the tyrannical boss lady. Erin giggled as she cited their speeches, all full of bravo, and then reported that they had decided to 'hold off' just another week or two, as word was that changes were coming soon and all would be taken care of. I laughed, for word of impending changes made the rounds everyday and nothing was ever done.

So that is how I was undone. Or rather, I undid myself as my inner resentment grew. There was no let-up in the work. But Erin's inviting smile, her casual playfulness, those catty eyes, were too much for me. There at the company, down the hallway to a locked door, we slipped away and into a dark office to fumble with our clothing. Laughing all the while, knocking a file cabinet, noisy then hushed, excited—so excited—half-naked, then moaning and caressing each other, the door opened, the light shone in, and the hideous fat face appeared.

36.

I was fired from my position at the top company. Just like that, although they'd apparently been giving me warning signs and I'd been oblivious to them, too caught up in the joy I knew and brought to others daily to suspect I'd overstepped the boundaries, carried this joy thing too far. Even joy, I suppose, must be contained. There is a time and a place for joy, just as with everything else, and you cannot impose joy on just any situation. Joy is rebuffed in most business atmospheres and at the dentist and especially if you run out of gas on the freeway. There is no place for joy in these instances, even if you happen to feel joy then. Have you ever known those peculiar occasions, where you're walking along, or sitting doing nothing, and for no particular reason you are overcome with a good feeling, a kind of sparkling contentment? You search your Rolodex of recent experiences and you can't locate a reason—no lotto winnings, no job promotion, not even better mileage on that last full tank of gas. You wonder where in the world this feeling came from, and why. The marvel is that you enjoy it for the moment. People (philosopher-types) make up songs about these moments— Oh happy day! Forget your cares, c'mon get happy! Don't worry, be happy! And these little ditties, suggested by no more than a moment of unexpected joy, inspire millions, the whole world.

What if the creators of these song-poems had been told to curtail their joy, or get over it and get back to something serious and more practical? Well, that's what I was told basically, or rather, I was told to take my joy elsewhere. Apparently it wasn't as infectious as I'd thought. My real mistake, though, was failing to write it down, capture it in a few catchy verses so the world could know how I felt. I was simply not a good enough capitalist to suspend the personal rapture I felt long enough to consider it as a marketable commodity. It also didn't help that I had no past experience as a tunesmith. But though I was shocked—stunned really—to be let go from the huge, well-respected company, the true jolt was yet to come. Simply put, when catastrophe arrived and wiped out joy, it did so thoroughly, and it was only then, at that moment—that earth-based, shallow, egocentric, mundane worldly moment (where catastrophe resides)—that I lost sight of the miracle that had summoned me and transformed me, and I fell back into the persona I'd previously known—except that now I was tinged with despair, and moving incrementally away from the joyous vision which had changed me.

The joy having been knocked right out of me by my dismissal, my relationship with Erin took on a worldly face full of doubt. For the first time I began to notice things I'd overlooked about her, how she chose the most expensive places to dine and always ordered the priciest dish, then failed to eat even half of it. She arranged outings and excursions I didn't care for, but that cost a pretty penny (there is no such thing; it's only an expression for a much larger amount of money). She brightly and prettily—for that was her way, always peppy and pleasant—suggested gifts for herself and nudged me into buying them for her, while leading me through boutiques and commercial squares I'd never bother with alone.

I hadn't paid it all much mind when the job was there and the pile of wealth was high. But now I'd been relieved of the paying position and for the first time I looked at Erin as an expense. I let the money go, go, go to her, but inside I was not as calm, not as indifferent to money as I'd been before. I, who had lived on nothing, who had prided myself as opposite the wage earner mentality, was now too much cognizant of my dwindling resources. What would I do, what would I do, I wondered, when the money was gone? That question had never occurred to me when I'd had nothing at all. What about the enrichment of a new thought, blue water and green grass, the sparkling awe of just being alive? Where had the value of all that thinking gone? I considered myself some lousy hypocrite, but that only added to my unease. I was nervous, truly nervous, about some impending personal doom, when in fact I'd lived with certain doom all my life and barely paid it any mind. I saw a changed expression on Erin's face, as if she knew what I was headed for, as if perhaps she was leading me there, and inside I understood I was about to be dropped off in a desert.

It was no surprise then to realize and admit to myself that I didn't love her, but had been consumed by a sensation larger than me, a revelation that I suddenly could no longer comprehend or understand. I felt like I'd been launched on some inner odyssey, and that now I'd crashed upon craggy rocks and could not remember my way, could not even recall why I'd set out on such a journey. I longed for my homeland, the safe, secure past, as I had known it, uninterrupted by pretensions to immortality, untouched by the truth of universal love. Worst of all, I saw no relief, no rescue, and no redemption in her. She was only a victim of my insane metaphysical tangent. In modern jargon you'd say, ah it just didn't work out, she wasn't the one for me, time to let go, move on, head our separate ways. But a curious grieving permeated me, a grieving for her.

I considered myself unworthy of happiness. I believed I had failed her, not as a lover, but as a human being. I did not know it then, but this was a good, true step, for soon I came to understand that I was right. I had indeed failed as a human being, and not on a personal level, but on a universal level. How is this good, you ask? How is this true? It showed me that what I was working on was not a personal relationship, but my relationship to the universe at large. It left me with an undiscovered ray of hope deep inside.

Now I have come around to the present moment, do you see? I have a ray of hope, an increment. Despair played its part out for me, nudging me down, down, to the black abyss. But the blacker it got the clearer became the glow of my one last ray of hope. I am here on the edge of the abyss now. That is where I am speaking to you from. If the page goes blank you'll know that I fell in, was swallowed up, consumed (it's just another tube, really, a scarier one, that's all). But as of this moment I am slowly working my way back to the incredulous vision of joy I know exists for anyone who wishes to see it. I just need to connect a few more dots.

PART 3

37.

Now perhaps you understand my position in life—I have two court dates, one for the overdue ticket and one for disturbing the peace in front of a public theater showing "Rent." You might also be wondering what more a blithering idiot such as myself can possibly say. Haven't I said it all by now?

I told you how I enjoyed myself right out of my job, how I loved the universe so completely I nearly destroyed an innocent girl, and how I then drove a disintegrating bomb through streets and into parking lots until the thing betrayed me in heavy traffic. I recounted how I walked and walked and roamed and slept outside, all the while forming a closer bond with this great good mysterious overmind that is everywhere all at once. Yes, I told you all of that and how I eat cardboard and feel like an ant and how the inside of my head shows up in the outside—all in an attempt to illuminate this spiritual journey I'm on, that we're all on, really.

Well, isn't that enough, you must be wondering, and cringing at my answer—that no, I'm not done, that my purpose is to fully re-integrate myself back into the world, but as one who reached the edge of the abyss and looked in, then almost slipped in, but instead, clung to a particle of light and fought his way back. Didn't I tell you that I had one of those TV movie-of-the-week tales that went from normal life to near death and then resurrection from the ashy throes of failure? Do you think that, after all I've been through, I will be satisfied to merely wander like some ninny, forever (and ever) possessed of the secrets of the universe while subsisting on pennies and associating with gnats? No, there is more to me than that, much more.

I have reevaluated my relationship with this grand mind that contains me. I'm sorry to report that some of my earlier musings may have been a bit off the mark. I regret if I've misled you or caused you, yourself to abandon your normal way of life and consider mine a more appropriate way to exist. I know I said I felt blessed and sacred and intimately in touch with the worldwide mind, which is everywhere, within everything, inescapable, the true reality.

It's all true, to a certain point. But really, look at me, a broke, meandering, puzzled soul, and I ask you, am I in any better condition than the rich and powerful? How can I consider myself looked upon with such favor when I have no boat or car or home, no fabulous bank account (earning high percentage rates), no stock, no retirement savings, no lakefront property. Aren't the people who have all those things in much better favor with the universe at large than I am? It has bestowed upon them many gifts and protected them from harsher elements of the world that might harm them. They have beautiful skin and air-conditioning and time to do as they please (though the idle rich and the very poor share that similar trait of free time, just different kinds of free time).

I must admit, at last, that my true status within this reality picture, as a molecule with legs, is not so sublime as I'd like to think. The minor good fortunes that do come my way are just that—minor—and I am a bottom feeder in the sea of life. Do you see what I'm getting at? I'm not refuting all that I proclaimed before, all that mush about being worthwhile and meaningful no matter how small, how minuscule, how much like a minnow I am. Rather, I'm surrendering to the obvious—that the largest, most swollen of personalities, bloated with goods and wealth, overflowing with merchandise, with homes on three continents, admired, respected, revered and celebrated, is just as worthy as me in the all encompassing reality that flows in and throughout everything. And more than that, he has better luck. Yes, there it is, I've said it, I'm not so lucky. My life is not so charmed. All this time counting my incremental successes, and the air filling my lungs, and each new day as victories has pacified me. If I were so fortunate, so connected to the metaphysical reality that permeates the physical one, why would I be forced to struggle so hard just to live? Aren't those settled in luxury looked upon more favorably than me? Isn't that the true nature of reality, that the real insiders, the ones with the secret knowledge of how it all works, how the pieces fit, how to connect the dots, are doing well, very well, cruising as they say, living it up, enjoying this trip, probably on their way to a great afterlife as well?

Yes, yes, yes it can all get depressing. I go in and out of belief and confusion. I think I am a sacred being and then I believe I'm pus. All because of the course of this life I'm living. In comparison to others (the rich and famous and surely deserving, as I've just said) it sucks, to put it plainly. But when I apply my personal philosophy I seem to see through it. But is my philosophy just a sedative of my own making, to keep me from splintering psychologically? Am I just a worm, a maggot, despicable, vile slime with thoughts? Perhaps if I struck it rich I would know the answer. Or perhaps I could simply ask rich people: "Are you more worthy, closer to true Good, than the poor?" If the answer is yes, would it work strictly on an income basis, say, over two-hundred thousand a year would be the bottom rung of Goodness, and then up from there? Half a mil a year would qualify one for the Silver Club Level and a million a year the Gold, up to Platinum and billions and so on. Billionaires must be closer to true Good than the rest of us, no matter how they got their money. (Would that be a factor, then, in the eye(s) of this all-knowing consciousness, this extremely humorous and deceptive and playful, mysterious sly poser called the Universe? If you were once evil and poor, and then had murdered for your billion dollars and gotten away with it, would you instantly be one with true Goodness, along with having that glorious new furniture and a gated estate with resident security force?)

These are difficult questions, but necessary. They suggest an awful possibility—that this universal mind may itself be evil; or worse, that it draws no distinctions between evil and good acts, that it has its own reward system based upon doing what is possible and taking what is there, exploiting consciousness, so to speak. As someone once said, "Everything is permissible." Only meek souls have drawn lines around permissible acts and labeled them good or evil. Bold souls overstep those lines, erase them, laugh at them and draw their own, to get what they desire here in life, get where they are going, get ahead of me.

I have decided once and for all (how did we get that term, and others that include "one" with "all", like "all for one and one for all", and "all-in-one" such a popular advertising slogan; even "every man for himself" selects the one from the multitude, and "me against the world" points up the same concept, and "out of many comes one" a religious phrase I think, and then of course there's one-stop shopping which is an answer in itself). But yes, I have decided to confront my landlady, to face my fear. That is another of the psychologist's tools, the admonition to face your fear, go directly toward the trouble that paralyzes you. Deliberately do the very thing that you shy from. The premise is that you'll find it not so scary after all, that you'll prove your fear to be hollow, and in that way you'll conquer fear. So, as much as I disdain psychologists and their insipid tools and dictums, I'm going headlong into fear. I suspect that particular advice didn't originate with psychologists anyway, at least not modern ones. I'm sure it was compromised from a much wiser source. I know Emily Dickinson wrote, "As we feared it, it came" pointing out how fear is powerful enough to attract the feared phenomenon to the unfortunate scared soul. That I completely believe. I tend to trust poets, even those with degrees. Too bad more good poets don't play guitar. Can you imagine if Walt Whitman had formed a band?

But I am on my way there, to my landlady's house—to my room now. I will settle this (once and . . .) Even though I owe her money, we will work something out. I wonder if it is even worth the trouble to collect my few belongings. When I think of it, I have nothing much of value, just some clothes and a roll-up mattress, a few papers, personal notes, and a pad I've jotted stray thoughts on, thoughts I'd become quite proud of, really, some late-night scribbling, but poignant and enlightening. They shed some light on this condition we're all in, this human condition, and I wouldn't want to lose them.

The walk up the hillside is taxing, but refreshing. I've already sweated through my present set of clothes many times over and one more film of perspiration won't make a difference. I don't recall it being so far, but perhaps I'm experiencing a little anxiety, knowing I'll see her and talk to her, with everything on the line. Everything, for me, does not amount to much, as I've explained. Still, the odd trembling is upon me as I trudge uphill. The climb does get a little steep. When I drove, my car (that unfaithful quitter) grinded and lurched the last half-mile and each time I worried I'd stall and roll backward, downhill, all the way to the flat city blocks. Momentarily, I am pleased to be absent that concern now, though a new one flashes before me. I, myself might falter, trip and tumble heels-over-head until I rolled to a stop.

By the time I sight the ancient fortress, its high roof between mossy trees, I am soaked cold around my neck and armpits. Still, I wobble upward. It sits beneath the slight mist that accompanies these hills, its expansive and overgrown yard surrounded by a stone wall of medium height and easy enough to climb over. That is the way I enter now, easing down into the thicket of brush that borders the yard's edge, peering out to see who or what comes or goes. But as usual it is silent, empty, eerie.

What is fear to Flex Ponderosa, I suddenly thought. I puffed up inside and pushed the branches out of my way and strode across the dead grass, in the shadow of the fortress. Flex Ponderosa didn't need to duck and zigzag tree to tree, press up against a wall, slip unnoticed inside, slink down a hallway, tiptoe upstairs. Flex Ponderosa marched forward with his chest out, head high, jaw thrust, adamant, rightful. Flex was in command; his will be done.

Inside I let the door swing closed behind me, not a defiant slam, but a definite woody click signifying my entrance to anyone who might be listening. But no one was. At least, no one was visible and no sounds formed other than my own breathing, which was loud. No flame burned in the fireplace. No notes came from the piano. No one took up a seat at the great long table in the adjoining stone dining hall.

I walked casually through, ever more secure of who I was and what I wanted (though under a moment's examination these things would be revealed as not much, and . . . not much). I stood in the window of the living room, a perfect target, out in the open. Where was she? I hesitated only another second before starting upstairs to my room in the far upper corner of the north end of the fortress. I didn't really feel that I was facing my fear—my fear hadn't shown. That was a peculiar one, to finally get the nerve to plunge headfirst in at the deep end, only to find there's no water in the pool. Well, I was resigned, after all, to giving up this life on the run and meeting my creditors, my persecutors, my demons, whoever. I was ready to take on all comers, if only to allow them to bash and beat the living hell out of me, to mentally and physically flog me. I was simply tired, that's all. A mind reaches a place where it has tried and tried, gone round and round, theorized and figured and exclaimed "Aha!" and re-thought and calculated and thought, "Oh no." It reaches a place where it's sure it has the answer, and another place (maybe the same place) where it can't remember the question. The fatigue of existence has set in on me and there is no more winning or losing, no more catastrophe or joy, no more hope or despair. There is only an undeniable need for rest, a longing to surrender.

I reached my door and it stood open. Inside was the surprise that the universe loves to play, always waiting for the most unexpected moment, the most unexpected circumstances, the strangest time and place, catching one off guard (if one has ever been on guard, and I was one who had been on the lookout for coincidences, omens, signs, portents, all the visible stirring of an invisible world).

There she was, crouched over and reading, of all things, reading my words from my notepad, my private and extremely personal musings on the nature of this union we all have with the one entity we all form. Her hunched figure sensed me in the doorway, stood quickly, straightened and turned to face me and I nearly melted, for it was not the bug-eyed, crooked nosed, gray-haired landlady but the wispy, ethereal blond girl of beauty I'd seen fleetingly in the upstairs hallway on one other occasion.

I suddenly didn't mind that she was peeking in my private corner. Instead, I was pleased, thankful at last that someone else knew what was going on inside my head (even though what I'd written was all about how everyone—at some level—knew everything about everybody else, how it was all contained in the vast being that we all comprised, this ever-evolving thing that disguised itself in so many different ways, as me, as you, as her).

But as I have confessed already, I'd reached that stage of thought-rot where I could no longer analyze, abstract, deduce and conclude. I wanted only to let the forces about me, in and throughout me, above and below me have their way. I wanted to be pushed over the edge, blown to the four corners, drowned in the depths, stirred into the mix and poured out only to be sucked in and digested again. I bowed down (bent, really) to the Great Tube. But in a flash (I couldn't help it) I saw the possibility—that she was the one.

I had realized the value of this life and tried to achieve it with Erin, tried to love her, tried when it should have been easy, effortless, and real. I understood now what love wasn't. I had briefly entertained its potential with the Asian lady in the red dress down at City Hall, thinking surely I had come in contact with her expressly for the most important purpose of my life (for no meetings are accidents and what else could an encounter with such an attractive woman be for?). In a microsecond (small things are fast) it flooded me all over. I had come face to face with it at last, there in my own room (though I was behind on the rent) and I was in such a state, a state of reception, of willingness, of welcome, exhausted from the struggle, confused to the point of clarity, that I smiled.

38.

Well, I am wrong again, what's new about that? Of course she wasn't there for me, wasn't meant to meet me, wasn't destined to receive my one true universal offering. No, no, no. Didn't I tell you (I'm sure I did; I'm telling you everything) that it has me, I'm caught here, in its web, and it's watching me (watching all of me) while I can see only a tiny bit of it. I'm at its mercy and I'm the only one who doesn't seem to get it. It's everywhere I turn and there's no use pretending anymore. I cry out and it answers. I reach out and it takes my hand. I curl up inside and it's here with me. But why must it tease me, be so provocative, offer me fruit and serve me wax?

She was in my room, she told me, at the request of the landlady, who had taken ill and was in bed. She had been asked to find my copy of the lease, that's all, and she hadn't read anything. That's what she said, that she hadn't read a thing I'd written. I almost moved my tongue to beseech her to go ahead, please, read every word, I want you to. I almost did. Before I knew it, she proclaimed she had the paper. But instead of taking it, she handed it to me, said she had to be going, and that I should take it to the landlady myself, as it seemed we had some things to talk over. Then she was gone, just as she'd disappeared so easily that one other time in the upstairs hallway, out the door and down the steps as if walking on air. Gone. Bye-bye love; bye-bye happiness (sad songs also hold truth) and I stood clutching the paper in my hand.

What was it for, that meeting, I wondered? Why had I met the alluring Asian lady in the red dress? Why, what for, in each case, if not for the miracle of love in my life. No, only for another pinch from my impish companion who dwelled everywhere at once—all seeing and all knowing—and more of a practical joker than they ever taught you in church Catechism. That was always a tough one to figure as a kid—that omniscient, omnipresent stuff. How could he be everywhere at once, and know everything, too? I couldn't understand that. It seemed to take an awfully busy mind. Usually I would imagine he could see me, and a few others, on up the block and around the corner, and then I'd lose focus. If he was looking over there, how could he be looking over here, too, at the same time? And there were so many people and places so much further away, a whole planet full. It was beyond comprehension what they said he could do. But now it seems simple. There's less mystery. I believe I understand. Rather than a separate "he" who must try and be everywhere at once and know all things, "he" simply is the everywhere, and "he" is the everything. He's that big. Understanding this makes it clear that "he" could not possibly be unaware of a single thing, and could not possibly be absent from a single place. I am a single place, too, by the way. Now I must take my copy of the lease and face my fear, a slight woman confined to a bed.

I had the advantage, I knew, and the advantage over an enemy is a confidence booster. On the short walk downstairs, out through the rear kitchen door and across the overgrown courtyard to the landlady's modern home on a trimmed section of lawn I felt a temporary boost, based upon her being ill and probably unable to deal with me on her usual harsh terms. Instantly, though, it dissolved, when, after a considerable number of knocks with no response, I peeked in the front door.

She had deteriorated badly in only a short time. She was asleep and hooked up to an oxygen machine. An arm hung limply off her daybed. Labored breathing was punctuated by a phlegmy cough. Instead of standing triumphant over her diseased body, which looked like it might give out soon, I was struck by the appearance of such a combative and demanding soul reduced to this state. A wave of pity overcame me and I did not even consider that I might be able to name my own terms for reclaiming my room now, that

I could easily bully her into withdrawing the unfair charges for utilities, that I could win by using a power play, the way any good businessman in such a situation would act. I'm afraid I lacked the killer instinct, a fatal personality flaw when negotiating.

I stood over her for a while staring down at her wrinkles and emaciation. I hadn't realized she was so thin, bony really. This was the battle-ax who chased me through bushes and stood blocking my stairway? This was the yapper who belittled my name, turning it from a marquee title into a parody of itself? This was my fear, reduced to forced breathing through a tube. She was so clearly just a tube herself now, air in and air out, life visibly pumping, threatening not to return with each exhalation. That is when it becomes clear what tubes we are, when there is nothing left but short breath. I looked down at her lying there. Just a short time ago she was animated, vigorous alive, even dangerous. That is when our tube selves are not so easy to discern as tubes. We strut about and raise our voice and make demands, all until we're forced to hurry to the bathroom and tend to our other end. I considered the lines in her face and the saggy folded skin of her arms. She was no longer something to look upon, if she had ever been. She was also not a beautiful old building worth preserving. She was a chore, a task, a bag of suffering. (We're all bags of suffering it's obvious only when smiles wear off and panic appears in the eyes.) She was someone's responsibility, their job or their burden or both.

I wondered if she had family, relatives. The inside of her home looked like it had been clean and neat at some point. But clutter filled space between chairs in the living room; clothes draped their backs. A tray of medicines stood beside her daybed. The TV was on but with no sound. A blanket had been tossed over the blinds, and had slid half off. The phone was on the floor. Newspapers sat unopened by the door, along with shopping catalogs. Several half-eaten meals were piled on the kitchen counter, crumbs spilled, drink cartons left out. A wall calendar had days marked off up until the middle of the month. I didn't know what day it was, if or when the marking had ceased.

While I waited for her to awaken, I read my lease. But my eye wandered back to her and back to her and then settled on her. This was a human being in the final stage. She could not possibly have much time left. Sitting there stupidly, in an armchair littered with napkins and empty pill bottles, I had another of my incongruous thoughts. I wondered if anyone had told her they loved her. The only times I'd seen my landlady were first in brief business encounters when she'd shown me the room and I'd taken it, and subsequently in fleeting moments when I'd handed her the next payment, or I questioned the added-on charges and unimproved conditions about the great house. I had never had a personal chat with her and she had been steadily brusque and terse in manner. I'd never seen her accompanied by anyone, never noticed if a visitor arrived for her. She had been only a landlady to me, and then a persecutor, and I had so firmly set her in my mind (my world) in this role of adversary that I had not contemplated any other possible dimension of her life. In fact, as I'd contemplated my peculiar perception of the universe, she fit into it as a symbol for a loose end in my life, a completely unraveled part, where I'd come undone, gone off the deep end, fallen apart. I hadn't thought of her as "her" but as a dysfunctional part of me.

This particularly struck me as I sat watching her, for if she slipped away now could I characterize it as a quiet little victory for me, the last of a nagging sore in my otherwise colorful world? Gone would be a shrill voice, a debt. It would vanish and I could stand up and leave with no one to hold me back. Or I could stay out the remainder of days in my room, perhaps hide the lease and claim extra time to whomever might appear to take charge in her wake. I questioned whether the universe was set up for this exact kind of thing, an automatic last will available to those who decided they were beneficiaries. All I had to do to stake my claim was think, "yes."

The more I thought of this, as the landlady labored each breath, the more essential this question became. Was I going to allow her (and by doing so, allow everyone, allow all beings) her humanity,

her individual essence? Or was I going to relegate her to a part
played in my own private cosmos, a part that could be excised—a
cancer even—that would be to my benefit to have removed? Was
she a self, herself, or was she a part of me, a part of me I didn't
want? Either way, I justified, she was not a cardboard representation
of reality; she was true flesh and blood. The working theory I had
of all creation being a huge, monstrous, infinite mind did not
mean that what was within that mind was not real, was not solid,
was some sort of phantom reality. No, no, on the contrary, this
mind stuff was solid matter at every turn. But, Aha! This solid
stuff of the mind was malleable, by powers and contortions and
perceptions of mind, you see, a great gob of Play dough, or more
accurately Silly-Putty, and the hands that molded it, shaped it
from one object or person to the next were also Silly-Putty, as was
the molder-shaper behind the hands. All one, all one, all one, I
was Silly-Putty myself. I thought I felt a touch of fever overtaking
me as I sat so close to her in that disorganized room. Could I have
caught what she had?

That's when I thought of ending it for her. It would be simple,
really; disconnect the oxygen machine; place a hand across her
windpipe. It would be an act of mercy, really, for both of us. What
would be the consequences? In the real world, the hard, solid,
concrete material world I could slip out the door and no one would
know. She was ready to go and a breath or two sooner would raise
little suspicion. In the unreal world I would have my conscience to
deal with, and that would boil down to what I was talking about
before—is her death a symbolic plus for me, a sign that things
have taken a turn for the better, a small relief and change of direction
for me, one less anxiety?

So this, I pondered, must be the nature of a murderer's mind.
A murderer did not see it as a moral dilemma, but as a practical
decision, a path through this cluttered universe that must be cut,
one thing (or person) being no different from another (the stuff of
the universe like Silly-Putty, now shapeless, now a cow). The
premeditating murderer must be above normal, beyond notions

of good and evil, right and wrong, a most accomplished businessman in the only business there is, that of living and dying. So here was my opportunity to act upon my own theories. The question that occurred to me was, what would Flex Ponderosa do? For this was one of the big questions, and Flex was there to tackle gigantic issues.

But I did not get that far, for like two beacons from a netherworld her eyes fluttered open. They did not have much light in them and they rolled slightly, unstable. Her eyes focused at last on me sitting across from her, unaware that I'd been imagining her death in natural and unnatural ways. I half-expected the landlady to spring to her feet and jut an accusatory finger in my face, screaming "You! You! You!" I would hold up my lease and she would poke holes through it, shouting, "Pay! Pay! Pay!" I flinched at this idea, and then worried she'd seen that sign of weakness.

Opposite her in her sickroom now I fell nervous and uncertain. I was shrunken, muted, squashed. Humbled by "it" (that much larger, grand, infinite outgrowth of myself that extended forever (and ever) in all directions) surrounding me, I was stifled. The sheer scope of it, its immensity, its grandiosity came alive when the landlady opened her eyes. I laughed inwardly at the absurd notion that I could kill anyone. I couldn't kill a bug.

Once again I conceded my true proportions, minuscule really, and tried not to despise myself. I remembered that I had deemed even the smallest thing as sacred, as a necessary part of the infinite. Humility was a virtue. There was nothing to being big, to being immense. There was nothing to holding right and wrong, good and evil in the palm of your hand. There was nothing to considering it your privilege to decide who lived and who died. That was all a hallucination I reminded myself, a power trip for inflated egos. That was all misplaced hubris, enacted by souls who misinterpreted the permissiveness of the universe and thought they were the creators, the originators, the whole one instead of just one of the whole. I knew I was but a servant. I was a piece of God. Just a penny in a dollar—that was me, that was all of us—equal parts, equal.

You have to understand that these revelations and epiphanies concerning the nature of existence and why we're all here are difficult to keep in my head. The most amazing insight, a clear grasp of complex issues, the answers to big questions, all tend to dissipate, steam of the mind, unless they are concentrated upon and repeated inwardly on a daily, even hourly basis. Even then they fade, or if I can keep them alive and vivid, they leave no room for new realizations, just crowd my psyche with so much truth it's overwhelming. I've often found myself dissecting some inward mystery only to suddenly stop and gape and silently shout, "I know that already!" Yes, it's one I spent considerable time on long ago and it's over and done with—a known, a given, a truth.

But I can't help it. I cover much territory more than twice, many times over, over and over, as if flexing my mind and pondering the nature of being is, in fact, the answer and the reason and the truth all rolled into one.

I think too much. Really, this is exhausting. Just let me be happy.

A good pop song helps. "All you need is love" or something simple, very simple, "simple as A-B-C, do-re-me," easier and easier, "all is calm, all is bright," yes, and then 'yeah, yeah, yeah," and "fa-la-la" until there's nothing but pleasing grunts and monosyllables that we all know mean fun, contentment, ecstasy, joy! "Joy to the world!"

At that exact moment my landlady kicked me. It was not a malicious kick, though, just a nudge. She had no power in her foot and I could tell she was only trying to make contact. She gasped and tried to motion with a limp arm and I followed her movements, saw that the tube from her oxygen machine had become detached and she was getting no air. Here again the concept presented itself. What if I had not been in the room? What then? She might choke and slowly suffocate. I didn't know how dependent she was on the machine for her breathing. If I pretended not to know what she was gesturing at, I could get up and creep out of the house and who would know the difference . . . except me, of course, and we know by now, don't we, that that is all it takes. If I know something, then the entire living, pulsating, organic universe knows it (and this includes the dead, I'm sure, though I don't know how, I'm just convinced that there's nowhere else for them to be (or not be) than in this one jumbo mix; so she would know, yes, she would know).

Still, it wasn't out of guilt that I reached to make the connection for her. It wasn't out of fear of reprisal from an all-knowing and occasionally angry collective being. It wasn't even out of a sense of duty, or an act of kindness to a cripple or handicapped person. As I reached for that tube, to insert back into her tube (myself a tube, too, a tube who feels) I was possessed by emotion. I have said, and I stand by it, that we are sensitive, emotional creatures who can anticipate events and occurrences as they approach and before they happen. I'm saying that about all of us, as human beings, as a distinct characteristic of our species. That is our true nature. We are much more than brain containers who need food. We are tubes who feel, tubes who sense. This sense mechanism of ours extends beyond us—not invisible—but completely visible, for it is our own sixth (and seventh, eighth, ninth . . .) sense that we see when we look out at the world. Look closely and see more. Some of us already do that. Yes, I am one of them, and obviously, results are not guaranteed.

You can be driven crazy by this ability to know and understand what the universe at large is telling you at every moment. It is truly alarming, a paradigm shift, another world, not your usual day of work and groceries—though it appears to be a usual day, that's the trick; it's very subtle, right under your nose at all times. But, yes, I reached for the oxygen hose accompanied by an emotional vision born of compassion. This ugly, disintegrating creature who I'd likened to a thorn, this old, old very old and probably near useless thing that could no longer even collect rent due it, this unfair, unreasonable, unsightly and somewhat malicious being who I felt had been unnecessarily harsh with me was, in the most cosmic and eternal sense, due love.

39.

What a moron, what an imbecile you must think I am. I might even agree. But it all happened in a flash, a flash of insight, as I connected one tube to another tube. I knew then. Right then, I understood. I was done wandering, done waiting, done even with my social experiment of collecting pennies. I was finished with looking into the faces of every stranger, and especially every woman, who passed me on the street. I was through trying to ferret out my own personal connection in this limitless place of unending, countless connections (between all things, but only impersonally in my case). I was finished even with analyzing the day and night skies, the foliage of city parks, the patterns in tree leaves, the miraculous landscape just outside my own head (an extension of the inside of my head, I'm sure you remember) to determine exactly how I fit in (I didn't). I was done wondering Where's Waldo (me) in the intricate, overlapping design of the world, done trying to discern—as in that old TV game show "Concentration"—where the line of one object became the border of another object or of a person (me again). I was no longer going to spend my consciousness determining where you ended and I began, or vice versa. And I wouldn't be troubled by it anymore, for I had found my focus.

There is nothing like a purpose to take one's mind off of all that troubles him. A purpose in life is salvation, even if it's only an illusion, a false purpose, something you do to keep busy, or work. A purpose is an excellent time killer, or I should rephrase that, as, a purpose is an excellent use of time. Of course, many a purpose has been carried too far, taken too seriously. For religious purposes, millions die and millions suffer and there's a great deal of carnage and it all makes for history. But generally, if not treated too fanatically, a purpose is a good thing to occupy one for the eighty-odd years you're allotted as a conscious tube. A purpose, I should clarify, often overtakes one, enlists one, compels one, though the other way around is also possible, as one can decide a certain purpose suits him and then put all else aside and serve that purpose. In my own case, it was a combination of both. I saw my purpose in a flash, and then decided to dedicate myself to it. But truly, the dedication part wasn't much, not hard at all, nothing I had to concentrate upon and avow, it was automatic. I had arrived and I knew it. All my extra senses told me at once. My intuition cum metaphysical reality said it, portrayed it, right there in front of me. The landlady needed me.

I reattached her oxygen tube and voila! We were connected in a new way, not just cosmically, not even just personally, but intimately. Her gasping and twitching abated and she was able to gaze calmly at me with her soon-to-be otherworldly orbs. That's when I leaned forward, took her bird-like hand in mine and, placing my other palm atop it, cradled it like a precious jewel. Some skin came off and fluttered to the floor, incandescent flakes in the bright field of living room sun. Her hand so coarse and bony, could have been an animal claw, so brittle I might have crushed it had I not taken care. She was cold, too, but now I equated that cold not with the heart of stone I had formerly attributed to her, but with a spiritual need. I rubbed her hand slightly, patted it to warmth. Her pleasure was visible, palpable, reverberating through her tiny thin fame, a shudder of ecstasy. I wondered how long she had gone without being touched. She was like me, I thought, and at the same moment realized I, too, had been touched. Her scaly fingers trembled against mine; squirmed like hungry larvae and I knew a smidgeon of human response.

What a miracle a touch can be. We take touch for granted everywhere, everyday, even fend it off, avoid it, and abhor it. Others carry germs, or grease and grime, or they're unsightly, repugnant creatures that do not look at all like models in magazines or stars from movies and TV. Flesh is very choosy about other flesh. But one thing is clear—flesh needs other flesh. (The skin, after all, is the largest organ of the body, acutely sensitive, always reacting to the environs, and a force field for the heart.) When the flesh's need for other flesh is met, even in the smallest way, it revitalizes, re-ignites the soul.

Of course, much touching is impersonal and brusque. Handshakes among businessmen are apt to signify power, firmness and fortitude, not convey compassion. And abusive touch, violent and harmful touch, the strangling hands, the beating fists, these are perversions of touch. Otherwise, touch can be exquisite, and I basked in that feeling as I held the landlady's hand in mine, all thoughts dissolved, all else out of mind except what we both needed.

Hope, that incremental phenomenon, began again. It began again with a skinny collection of bones confined to a bed and unable to keep food down most days. Hope appeared in the dust that layered the landlady's home, her things, even the landlady herself. Hope exited the dust for the air that we both breathed and resonated in the humming sound of the oxygen machine, the quietude elsewhere. Hope had come not only for me but also for her and proved excellent company, nearly visible.

My days and nights became marathons of care interrupted only by the landlady's smiles or her snoring. There was much work to be done about the house, cooking and cleaning and straightening, and vital needs that had gone ignored, such as ordering medicines and administering them. This was tricky and required I draw up a chart, for she could only take some on an empty stomach, others with meals, certain pills at bedtime, and different pills upon awakening. A few had to be chewed, while some were too bitter or were capsules. In those cases I helped her sit up, rubbed her back and patted it and watched her swallow with difficulty.

The bathroom was a short hallway from her couch-bed but she could not make that walk. I lifted her onto her bedpan and off again, wiped her and dumped the contents, all as if cleaning up after the cat, an infirm one. Her odor and her stains didn't repulse me one bit. No, instead I accepted them at once, decided in a moment that this was humanity in its glory, tube-ness at its essence. It did occur to me to wonder, in a kind of grand way, who actually did clean up all the crap of humanity, seeing as how it flowed endlessly all the time. There was an absolute stream of crap, a river, an ocean of shit around us needing constant janitorial service. Whole industries were devoted to it, of course, but even after their efforts—there was still more, always more, behind each and every one of us, regularly. Obviously the job was never done. Cleaning up after our selves was a lifelong chore. But it was not for everybody. Most were better at making messes than attending to them. Funny that it should be considered such low work, the dirty work. Yet it was so necessary, essential. I saw that she was as good as dead without someone to do her dirty work. Apparently, we all are. Still, it is work assigned to fools, losers, the poor and unskilled. There is absolutely nothing noble about shit.

It had become clear right away that she had no visitors (the same as me). But there were tenants left in the old fortress who deposited their rent checks with a creaky lift of the mail slot in the bottom of the front door. Of course, I had no way of knowing if there was anyone still living in the castle-like house who had stopped paying rent or was in dispute over a utility bill, as I had not taken it upon myself to police the rest of the grounds. I had only interpreted the contented grunts and whispers of the old woman and done her bidding from the moment we both felt and understood the significance of that touch. It went unspoken that, if we had a debt to settle, if I owed for anything, if there was a past to answer for, it was all cleared away in the blaze of new hope that ignited the cluttered room, the un-stocked kitchen, both our lives. The landlady and her house became the center of my universe.

An intriguing notion, that this place was smack dab in the middle of the cosmic cyclone, for it was, in truth, as far from the madding crowd and the daily pulse of life as could be. But, just as some steady workers report day after day to large corporations and feel buried alive in the midst of suits and faces and passing co-workers in short skirts, the definition of every space on this all-encompassing reality board is open to interpretation. You may at any time feel way in, or way out, caught up in the life circus or ignored by it, an integral piece of the whole or a worthless crumb separated from the pie. I had wandered busy streets and peered into preoccupied faces finding nothing, nothing, and nothing. I spoke (only infrequently) to mannequins and imposters, cardboard receptacles of words, blank pads of pseudo-absorption, all the while confounded by the truth that we were intimately connected. It all seemed odd and absurd, a dumb show (for the words weren't real; no one spoke and no one heard) between strangers who would never open their vest to reveal there, unshielded by skin, a shuddering, beating heart ripe and red and around it an aura.

But as soon as that phenomenon occurrs—as with the landlady, who had shown me her heart and revealed a soul and I instantly knew where my own resided—the true connection is established and the space one inhabits becomes the wildest, dizziest, most intense and gratifying stratosphere (just as Earth itself is deep, deep out in outer space and there's no need to blast off to anywhere, we're already there, as I've explained). Yes, that's what happened, space came alive for me right in my own (the landlady's) backyard. The details and incidentals I dealt with were not chores, not obligations, but paths to the spirit. Handling medicines or monies (for the landlady had no capability for either and entrusted me to deposit her checks and withdraw her funds) I walked on air, friends with the great good universe.

After some time of this, wiping the spittle from the drooling landlady's chin, dressing and undressing her for the trip from the couch to the bed and back, watching inane re-runs of Gomer Pyle and The Beverly Hillbillies, raising the shade, lowering the shade, raising it, lowering, after scores of microwave meals and fruit out of a can, oatmeal and crackers and doughnuts (she really had a sweet tooth), of crumbs on the floor and in the cushions and leftovers and adjusting the air to cool, now warmer, now cooler, of draping her in a sweater for sleep and checking off the pills she swallowed, after a routine was established, and broken, and repaired, and forgotten, after all this I had the glow in her eyes to satisfy me. In the same way that survivors of near-death experiences proclaimed the Lord had been with them in their time of need, had indeed saved them (no matter who had caused their plane to crash or boat to sink or car to flip), I felt that the unseen hand whose fingers were everywhere had pointed me in the right direction and here I was, fulfilled in the company of this dying woman.

I had connected one dot. I had connected my dot to her dot. Isn't that enough? Is that enough for a TV Movie of the Week? Is it enough for you? Is it enough to touch an entire television audience, perhaps elicit a tear? Remember, I was at the edge of the abyss, about to fall in. I could have been in an eternal black hole, some infinite spin cycle, I was that close. I had been reduced to making friends with a gnat. I could have wasted the most essential element of a human being—the essence that is me. Instead I resurrected it (from its burial in the midst of humanity, its internment right out in the open) and discovered new life, love, and hope—joy! Mine is a tale of survival against the odds, warranting a song of my harrowing journey. "I been through the desert on a horse with no name . . . " and the sampling of someone's resilient overture "If I can make it there, I'll make it anywhere . . ." yes and visions of a better future "I'm going where the sun keeps shining, through the pouring rain," to "beyond the blue horizon lies a rising sun . . ." (These are but soundtrack suggestions and if my story is told on the tube or even on the big screen, I will settle for any small technical advisor role, or a minor part (perhaps as myself) an extra or a moving piece of the background.) Of course, my story was constructed on menial tasks and daily minutiae, the inconsequential of life, the absolute ennui of existence. Yet I felt it possessed certain heroics. I don't think I would be going too far to portray myself as a hero. It is not out of the question, not outlandish. I have endured and survived an ordeal by blowing on a spark of hope one millimeter the size of a match flame. Give me credit for that (screen credit).

I am attempting to come full circle now—around to triumph, success—from the beckoning grave. I had a foot in and yet I ended up dancing upon it. That's the stuff we like, scary reality that threatens to collapse inward until the hero (me) rises up and (with the help of the gods) overcomes. In my victory, I prove that Good defeats Evil, that it's all worth it (this life struggle) that we are not here for nothing, that there is a purpose (yes, that keeps us going) and even a greater fulfillment beyond this temporal life, a fulfillment that we can know at least a part of now, one that we sense is enormous in its purest aspect. The general contentment from a tale of this magnitude leaves us floating. Do you think I have two hours' worth?

40.

While the landlady slept deeply, as she did for hours upon hours sometimes, I wandered the grounds and sometimes entered the great castle of boarding rooms. My own needs I'd confined to the floor of the landlady's house, where I'd fashioned a bed of discarded couch cushions and rolled sheets. I ate my meals with the landlady, who often spilled her portions, chewed noisily, spit out pieces she disliked or refused an entire plate, pleading no appetite. These actions, judged insufferable by most people, only endeared her further to me. The more she needed me, the more needed I was, you see.

One of my favorite chores was getting her something sweet the moment she desired it—a cake or doughnut or some pie. The keys to her luxury car hung on a hook by the door. It locked and unlocked automatically and provided a ride as if on a cloud. I'd coast down the hill in the fine, spotless, air-conditioned and well-appointed Lexus, nearly melted into the seat, buy an iced vanilla cruller and drive the lush, silent vehicle back up the hill. Let me reveal, however, my anxiety at being seen in such an expensive, desirable automobile. I could feel the eyes of lesser drivers (those in little tin cans, with stick shifts or no ac) as I glided past. I almost rolled down the (full power, electric) window and yelled to each one, (there were so many) "It isn't mine! I'm doing a poor old woman a favor, that's all!" But I hesitated, not wanting to draw additional attention. (Imagine, me, the invisible man of yesterday, now warding off all the eyes.) There was also an undercurrent I hadn't known before, a probability that had never bothered me. I could be attacked. I hadn't thought of it at all in so long. Even when I worked for the company and brought in good money, I was undecided on what to buy and didn't own much (certainly not the right clothes). I didn't carry wads of cash with me, just had it direct deposited to my one and only (ever) bank account.

But this, this car, this modern-day royal carriage was too much to hide. Even if I didn't own it, it was clear I was driving it. If someone—a carjacker, a thief, a violent predator, some troubled inner-city drug addict, a kid with a gun, one of the dangerous multitudes (included in the multitude that I considered an extended part of me)—wanted it, then I was an instant (and maybe easy?) target. This caused me an evasive action—I managed to find one of the few, if not the only drive-thru windows for doughnuts.

Upon returning to the castle-house with its majesty and its sprawl, its many windows and the tasteful charm of its architecture (it was an old place, one of the admired old places) another notion startled me. This house itself was a visible display of wealth, of ownership, of a position in life above the basic, the hand-to-mouth, paycheck-to-paycheck life so many led. It startled me for a moment to think that the landlady was no longer in charge here. Who was? Well, she was the owner and all of it was in her name, but I had assumed a kind of responsibility. It was only in my effort to connect with another, to do the right thing in a very confusing and maze-like universe that I had become attached to this piece of property.

As I mentioned, I'd taken the time to stroll about the great house and yard and nearly gotten lost among its many twisting stairways, winding paths, narrow hallways and rooms within rooms. I had also discovered that the house contained objects d' art (I felt comfortable using that phrase now that I belonged in the impressive palace). Along with the piano (which would be difficult to steal, I admit, but still . . .) were some paintings at intervals in the long upstairs hallways on the opposite end of the fortress from my old room. I couldn't discern their value, or if they were originals or fakes. But then, neither could some potential intruder, I assumed. Surveying the grand place—for security reasons—I noticed that some of the empty suites had lush carpet. I stepped upon this brand new cushioning, compared it to the tread-worn rug in my own garret at the far end of the house and got uncontrollably hot, before concluding that the landlady had been in the process of remodeling and my area was next.

Other doors were locked and the house was curiously silent. The large communal kitchen downstairs was free of traffic. Only a water jug and jar of applesauce were in the fridge, some tea bags in a cabinet. I had the unique sensation of being a ghost drifting about as I looked around the old place. What would become of all this when the landlady passed? I did not know if she had a will, or a living relative, or an outstanding mortgage. I did understand, though, that property was traditionally, rightfully kept in the family, and that's where money stayed, generation after generation. Those that had something in life made sure their heirs benefited, and so down through time rich families remained rich, poor families remained poor. The lucky ones were born into material comfort and established accounts. The rest of us better look in the want ads. But the notion did tickle me that, perhaps, with no one else in the picture, I would be the one to inherit the landlady's estate, and perhaps any bank holdings, if she were to die now. I was not ignorant or uninformed. I knew official papers were needed with signatures and notaries and all that. Nothing could be done without questioning from bank agents and lawyers. I didn't imagine engineering a scheme to name myself in a will or trust; quite the opposite, I couldn't care less. I only thought of it and dreamed for a moment that the landlady might want it that way.

Maybe there was nothing I could do about it, if she was determined that I collect everything when her end came. Perhaps she had secretly drawn up the papers already. She and I enjoyed a cozy association; far from the antagonizing cat-and-mouse ploys we worked on each other in the recent past. I micro-waved her TV dinners and sat beside her as she coughed up half her food. She smiled as I wiped her with napkins and fluffed her pillows. Our talk was not limited to the weather and what time it was or her medicines and shows (re-runs of Bonanza were a favorite). But I found I was comfortable with this kind of mindless banter for the first time in my life now that I had a purpose to accompany it.

She called me Flex, though I doubt she recognized me as a former tenant who owed on a utility bill. Her name was Mary, but I shortened it to Ma. I could have taken everything she had and walked out the door. But I didn't. I had found a purpose and knew that to be more important than easy wealth.

During her long naps I began making repairs to the old castle-house, patching holes in the walls, nailing baseboards together, washing grime from windows. I discovered a shed by the decrepit pool with tools and a lawnmower and I worked the yard into shape. While I mowed and cut and chopped and raked I couldn't help entertaining my little daydream. What if it all became mine? I would do nothing to hasten her death and not even make a suggestion to her on my own behalf. Still, who else was there? It was a heady thought. I could bring them all here, my drug-addicted family, and they could each select a room for themselves in the great house. There were plenty available and I wouldn't force any tenants out.

The pool bubbled lively blue now that I'd sifted the leaves and algae out and activated the pump. The yard sparkled green. I'd found my blue water and green grass and it would be like a health spa to the addicts. I was electrified inside, my long mission finally pointing toward its conclusion, and a successful one at that. They would all recover here, regain their sense of themselves, become whole again. Briefly, I thought I could treat other drug-dependent, washed-out souls, and imagined a lawn full of the reborn, all stretched healthily out on chaise lounges in the invigorating sun, recharging. It could be turned into a weekly, prime-time TV series called "Your Day in the Sun" with me as the host and rotating guest stars playing nearly destroyed personalities who put it all back together at my retreat. (We could use real stars, with real drug problems!) That is what I mean by coming full circle, around from the black abyss to Number One in the ratings! What a story I'd have. If not a continuing series, at least a special, right?

41.

Well, all right the police are here for me and now I see things won't work out quite as I expected. I don't know who called them. It was not my landlady. I know that. But they are knocking at the door this moment.

I should tell you, before I answer their knocking, which has quickly grown to pounding, that these last weeks, or months—I don't know, I've lost track of time—that I've spent with Ma (Mary) have been as satisfactory as any in my life. I mean that in every respect, for beyond the simple daily chores I performed for her, and beyond the extra responsibilities I took upon myself out in the yard and in the castle house, and even beyond the obvious and genuine affection we shared—the infant-like smile she offered when I spooned oatmeal into her mouth—there was something more. In her most lucid moments, usually early in the evening, just past dinner but shortly before bedtime, in front of the constant glimmering TV screen showing some rerun or game show she enjoyed, we talked. We really talked.

Possessed of her faculties after a decent meal and enjoying my company, the landlady and I had many deep and enlightening conversations about the meaning of it all, the miracle of life, the way faith provided sustenance, and the ever-intriguing mystery of existence. These were welcome subjects to one in her condition, one who did not have all that long to live and knew it. The rest of us are so sure we have gobs and gobs of time left that the essential topics can be put off and put off, rarely discussed or even addressed. We're all confident of a long life span and never expect to get caught in a restaurant robbery, hustled into a freezer room and shot in the head, or slide on wet pavement off a two-hundred-foot-high bridge into the drink. When it does happen (it's on the news everyday) I wonder what occurs in the minds of the victims in their last moment (precisely when they realize it's their last moment). Probably they think of their loved ones and try to remember if they said it. Did they say, "I love you" to the most cherished face they can recall? Perhaps some suddenly focus on an insignificant aspect, a door handle or a lock, a hat hanging on a hook, the image outlined in a cloud above, or even a blotch on their own skin, and a revelation occurs, they see finally that they've never looked closely at a door handle or a hat, never seen what's in a cloud or on their own skin, never . . . And then it's over—another missed opportunity. Luckily, the landlady and I had ample time to cover important topics.

The most startling discovery was mine, though, for I found that she agreed with many of my notions and concepts. After a lengthy and perhaps even convoluted explanation of the workings of the universe (as analyzed by me) she would nod enthusiastically, still chewing, and say, "Of course, of course," and "I know, I know." These were truly magical moments, interrupted briefly by the laugh track of some sit-com or by a particularly tough game show riddle which diverted both our attentions. But always, and during commercial breaks, we returned to what we were talking about, usually picking up the thread of the discussion right where we left off. When we didn't talk we reflected quietly, sitting in a meditative state for hours at a time, pondering, pondering, and I could tell our thoughts were similar, if not exactly alike. To think, all this time I'd feared and avoided this woman and here she turned out to be a kindred spirit.

She was also smarter than I'd realized. She understood the Void—that we lived in it, that all things lived in it, that, indeed, the irony of the Void was that it could never be empty, only full, but full only because it was empty to begin with. This may confuse you, but it didn't confuse her! She saw that emptiness and fullness was the same thing, that one presumed the other, that the background was alive! I think she understood so well due to her condition, her nearness to death, to supposed emptiness. She saw that she was really going nowhere, (as we all are) that she already was nowhere, (as we all are) that nowhere is an emptiness so complete that it is filled with everywhere—you see?—only complete emptiness can contain everything. I don't know if the police understood this concept. They were nearly breaking the door down now, shouting, and proclaiming their official right to enter.

42.

The first policeman on the scene informs me that they have already looked through my room and confiscated my notes and that he has read them. He laughs and tells me what he thinks of my ideas and theories. He disagrees with me on almost every issue, he proclaims, without going into detail. He says I'm suffering from delusions and there may be good reason to hospitalize me, that is, if I'm not sent to prison. He alludes to a few passages in particular and I can see he's holding photocopies of them, of my own scribbles, (I have to admit a touch of pride here, that someone would copy my work) and he comments that I'm lucky the landlady is still alive or there might be enough evidence to convict me of murder.

He waves pages where I remark upon the uselessness of old things. I explain I was talking about buildings. He says, "Sure you were," with the air of a man who has heard a million and one alibis. In any case, though they have seized me and handcuffed me, I am not at all concerned. I turn to Ma and smile, hoping she isn't upset and alarmed at what they're doing to me. She doesn't seem all that bothered, which is good, but also bad, and I try and discern the look on her face. But she's chewing a piece of bread and butter I'd prepared for her and I can't tell what she's thinking.

"She'll tell you," I state confidently.

"You know this fellow?" The policeman asks Ma.

She looks bewildered, but happy to have company.

"Tell them how we watched the Bonanza marathon, Ma—"

"Quiet. No help," says the cop.

"What day is today?" asks Ma, one of her standard questions.

"Friday, Ma'am," says the cop.

Ma takes a moment to digest that.

"We've received information that this guy's been using your car, eating here and perhaps doing your banking, Ma'am—" starts the cop, and I see right away what he's getting at. I relax, as Ma peers for a moment at the remains of her doughnut. Then she looks the cop right in the eye.

"What day is this?" she asks.

There's general commotion and I'm treated roughly in their hold for a moment, admonished for taking advantage of an old woman.

"That's not how it is—"

"What have you done with the money?" they're in my face.

"Do you know this guy?" they push Ma at me.

"No, I don't think so. But I'm pleased to meet you, sir—"

"Ma it's me, Flex!" I cry.

But at that second Ma swoons. Her eyes fail and she topples. I start for her, but I'm restrained. The policemen ease her back onto the couch and I see she is still breathing.

"It's okay, this has happened before," I hear myself say. "Ma is right on the line," I explain further, but the policemen are busy with official instructions to each other. One calls headquarters on a cell phone.

I repeat that she's right on the line, the line between life and death. In the silence, as they await instructions from headquarters, I go on and no one stops me.

What is the point of all that we do in this life if it's clear that life may be over at any moment? Is it really necessary for Ma to buy a new dress, order ruffled curtains from a catalog, get the car washed and tuned up if she is about to go in the next breath, or the next? Is it worth it to select the higher priced can of vegetables because they're a better brand, or to play the Lotto if today might be her last day? Should she bother even having the laundry done, the dishes washed, her teeth brushed when it's a certainty she won't last the month, good odds two weeks is the limit, a bet that this week will be the end, a probability today is the day, a possibility the hour is near? It is a delicate question, I assure the policemen who appear to be listening to me, even taking notes. Is there a specific time where we let it all go, say "enough", concede that fate and rot and world-weariness have at last gained the advantage and shopping is no use, no fun? When do we abandon the actions of the world and fall back upon the machinations of the universe? How is that moment determined, and who decides? Is it left up to the person who is about to perish? There's a chance that crazy old grandma, on her deathbed, will go rabid with material lust, eyes alight with greed and a sudden understanding that she can have all she wants, that the grandchildren's trust fund is still hers, until the lights are out. So quick, bring the Sears Catalog and J.C. Penny and get this and this, and send that and that! Whose duty is it to limit her spree? Is there a duty? Should she keep piling up the goods and objects until her eyes freeze and go blank? What about her meals? Three full ones a day with required amounts of protein and carbohydrate, though we know that nothing will save her? Even a condemned man is guaranteed a final full dinner of his choice. The point? The point of it all? I see that question in their eyes. Yes, I'm getting to it. But then the phone barks and I'm cut off mid-sentence. One cop stares in my eyes.

"You're a cold bastard," he says.

"No, let me finish," but they're scrambling about now, not listening. I want to tell them the point. The point is, I shout, but they shut me up. The point is, I mutter, that she is entitled; Ma is entitled. They, we, even I, we're all entitled to the trappings of this material life right up to the final tock of the clock. We're due respect and most importantly, love. That's when I'm hit, slapped hard across my mouth, when I utter the word "love" and the cop hears me. He growls that I have no right using that word and cocks his fist ready for me to say it again. I'm only trying to finish what I was saying, I plead, that a bell does not go off signifying "It's over!" when the designated sick person or old person is judged no longer worthy of receiving the same valuable goods and services the rest of us clamor for day after day. (When I say the rest of us, I don't mean me, of course. We know by now that I don't need or want any of the nonsense that makes up most lives.) But it's no good and I'm hustled off to a waiting police car. Still, I give it one more try.

"When do we give up on a human being?!" I scream. "When do we say they're not worth it anymore, not worth the price of a new sweater, not worth the price of a steak and lobster combo, not worth the price of new carpeting? When is it over, when the afflicted one is right on that line between life and death? Do we allow them less, because of less time to live? Is that the standard by which all shopping is done? The more time you (think you) have left, the more you're supposed to accumulate, and the less time you have (according to doctors' prognoses) the less stuff, really, you should acquire (certainly no long-term investments). Perhaps there should be a cut-off time for full-time shopping, say age 70, so that one tapers off the buying. But really, where's the value placed—on the person or on the new car?"

The cop's hand muffles me, surrounds my mouth, pinches my nose, cuts off breath, purposely. I know it's on purpose and I can't help kicking, spasms, it's my lungs convulsing. I need air! Now three of them are on me. "Aaaaaahhhhh!" I get my mouth open and suck the great invisible. "Uuuuuuuuhhhhhhhh!" Oh, the relief! I hardly feel the blows and grip on me, just luxuriate in the air, wonder how I could take it for granted every day, every moment, just because I can't see it. I want to touch it and hold it like I would a spoiled puppy. I focus on my lung full and hold it swimmingly an extra half-beat, caress the gorgeous stuff while it fills me. Oh air, air, oxygen! Imagine the longing for it when you're down to your last, your very last inhalation. What you would give for it then, this magical nothingness, everywhere, everywhere but in you, to die for! Choose quickly there at the end, choose, the brand new dress, or air? The shiny Lexus, or air? The blank check with your name on it, or air? Yes, air is undervalued. Get yourself full and replenished each moment, then move on and forget about it.

43.

I sit in a small cold cell. I am a small cold cell.

44.

They're letting me go. Just like that, I'm free. The barred door opens up and I walk through. The locked corridor springs open and I pass. Outside I look one way and the next. Are there only four directions? I suppose one of them is the right way. I take a step, hoping I'm right. Just one step away from the past and I feel it slipping, disappearing behind me. I had "it" once, didn't I? You know what I mean by "it"? I knew something, at some point, enough to grasp it, hold it in my hand, a truth. Yes, I believe I knew the truth. I figured it out, or stumbled across it, or someone told it to me, or perhaps it was for sale. But I knew it back then, a step or two ago. Is it possible to leave the truth behind? If so, what is it that I'm setting out for? Do we go round and round, discovering, forgetting, realizing again, losing it all, on and on, forever and ever, and ever? (Add as many evers as necessary).

45.

A spot of light. I believe I see a spot of light. It's perfectly clear that a spot is all I need.

The End

Printed in the United States
1187600001B/484

9 781401 002961